MW00398850

The Grisly Wife

Rodney Hall

THE
GRISLY WIFE

Farrar Straus Giroux

New York

Copyright © 1993 by Rodney Hall
All rights reserved
Printed in the United States of America
Published simultaneously in Canada by HarperCollins Canada Ltd
Designed by Cynthia Krupat
First printing, 1993

Library of Congress Cataloging-in-Publication Data
Hall, Rodney.
The grisly wife / Rodney Hall.
p. cm.
1. Australia—History—Fiction. I. Title.
PR9619.3.H285G75 1993 823—dc20 93-802 CIP

I acknowledge with gratitude

the help so generously given me by

Iain McCalman and Suzanne Rickard.

The Grisly Wife

Queer thing — but yes — we do mourn for the England we lost — maybe because the darkness of the tragedy awaiting us in New South Wales has left the memories of our youth bathed by contrast in clear simple light — and after so many years of exile one's gentler adventures tend to rise to the surface more and more appealingly —

But the day we set sail from Bristol I doubt if a tear was shed for home — England being so given to licence in those days and ourselves so out of step — I believe I speak for everyone including the prophet — this was to be our adventure in self-sacrifice and despite the fact that we were never exactly missionaries in the usual sense we did speak of this place as a mission right from the beginning — just as we accepted that we were the Chosen Few —

Being the Chosen Few meant we had a great deal more to look forward to than we had to look back on! — but *you* will never understand — no one born over here can have the least notion how desperate people were to escape the smut and futility of England then —

The whole enterprise depended on the prophet — the idea of the mission — the inspiration — the firm sense of being in contact with the Almighty — without the prophet's powerful personality the tragedy would never have been possible — oh let people say what they like about him being something of a weaselish specimen (I've heard it myself) and admittedly he does have a small face but a face simply filled with features — big ears big eyes high cheekbones thick brows — not to mention the perpetually big amazement of an individual determined to escape something in his past — something conceivably stupid — though once you startle him out of himself his eyes come so alive they astonish you and he can smile a whole gallery of teeth and show himself in a trice so handsome it hurts your heart to see his black hair gleam without a trace of grey —

As for his not being masterful — didn't he sweep us off our feet? didn't he gather us together as disciples? didn't he unite us as a family of women? — though he could neither read nor write didn't he succeed in firing us with his vision? wasn't the passage out merely part of his purpose? weren't we ready to faint when we first walked into that great draughty room at Bristol docks only to take comfort from the way he barked at the porters? —

I remember a salt wind blowing in from the open sea — mixed with a down-to-earth hemp smell — the blend intoxicatingly new to me — like the whiff of a fabled creature I had heard of but never encountered —

A clutter of heels knocked hesitantly on the flagstones while we presented our papers to company officials and fussed over the necessities of labelling baggage — echoes echoing in the heart — only to watch our pathetic few possessions trundled away on barrows through an archway where we glimpsed the ship's dark sea-stained timbers — with two sailors at a section of rail scouring the brass to sluice off an accumulation of rime —

The prophet did not flinch — even at the sight of that dismal tub and the way she diminished our future — and I trailed after him — though the odd fact is that we had no sooner climbed the gangplank than I was possessed by fierce regrets that the ship was not smaller and not more squalid!

Excuse me a moment — this country is too infernally *hot* for a person to draw breath!

The source of his power was a gift from God — an amazing talent — a secret — and I knew what this gift was — I had sworn never to tell — he bruised my arm when he made me swear so that's how important the secret was — until such time as he would need to come out into the open and use it to confirm a miracle —

How thrilling the future sounded then —

Still a girl and very giddy I used to whisper what I knew — always in the dark and always only to him — when I needed the comfort of reminding him how strictly I was keeping the news from everyone else — or if I needed to feel we shared something in our lives — he being my husband you see —

No sooner had we possessed ourselves of a berth each and gathered again on deck than Beatrice took issue with the prophet over his use of the word "ocean" and treated us to a disquisition on oceans in various biblical contexts   "For the entire *three* hundred years from 1611 to 1866 — " she pursued her theory through several translations of the Scriptures and enlarged on it with such impressive confidence that her cavils and polite contradictions once again drove him out of all patience — though she apologized as usual before proving him wrong —

And she did pay her own way it has to be said —

We guessed what was coming next because we knew her well though she had probably been with us less than a month at that time — and sure enough she proceeded to cite the true meanings of biblical symbolism (water as the symbol for people — day the symbol for a year or a thousand years — beasts for kingdoms — fear for love — and whatnot) — she was so positively fired with her own rightness she fell foul of Ann Whittaker too — you surely remember grumpy Ann who was such a saint underneath? —

Well there we were on board a ship and not one of us had even so much as glimpsed the open sea before —

It rocked about in a most sickening manner from the moment we cast off — sailors swarmed up the rigging to take their posts aloft like large dismal birds waiting for the tug to finish drawing us out into the channel where we were told we would catch a fine breeze — a fine breeze! — this violent wind slammed into us whistling among complicated ropes as the sails roared open and snapped tight —

The vessel thundered —

All passengers were ordered inside out of the way — so much for leaning on the rail at leisure to watch the Somerset coast dwindle while we fostered expected regrets concerning our recklessness! — the weather closed in almost as dark as night — "Night" Beatrice persisted breathlessly and coughing "steals on the house like" she coughed some more "like a murderer" — Ann sniffed — frantic sails began slatting — the mate who had welcomed us suavely at the companionway such a short time before now let loose halloos in a wolf's voice — the elements sent a violent thrill through the boards — "All snug!" a sailor bellowed back right in my ear — the ship already sheered along a swell though we had not yet reached the Atlantic — the tall clumsy apparatus tilting dangerously — an unbelievable volume of water gushed past driving regular crests to slap its hull hard and send spray whipping at our backs as we retreated to the saloon door — we plunged in among scores of frightened gentlefolk stopping their mouths with handkerchiefs while a few experienced colonials strutted from table to table offering words of comfort (such as "This is nothing to what you may expect!") and sipping punch —

Out there wild whistles shrilled from every direction as men galloped along the deck thudding past on bare feet —

I felt an urge to be in the open to face the danger so I elbowed my way back to an exit where the prophet and two stewards tried to restrain me — struggling with the brassbound door I slipped out despite a fierce funnel of wind — the hail of icy spray instantly shocked all breath from my body — I clutched at a deckchair rack to save being flung overboard —

Already drenched and thrown off balance and with drops of water dangling from my eyelashes I watched gangs of men rush helterskelter to humour the gale —

The masts had become useless tons of timber pitching about for no better purpose than to throw off any clinging sailors left up there fighting with canvas thick as wet carpet — this is what I saw before my mantle collar flipped up and blinded me forcing me to turn aside for the wind itself to free my face whilst I lurched back to safety — even then I only just managed to grasp the handle in time to avoid falling and rolling under the rail where the next wave would surely sweep me away —

The men who had stood peering out through salt-spattered glass assisted me in over the step meanwhile loudly condemning my folly — I dare say I looked a sight trembling and staggering about with hair plastered flat — then because the whole company mutely accused me of irresponsibility I cried aloud "I've never felt more alive!" — a fat lot of good that did me.

Well thanks to a courageous crew we hung on as far as Madeira where the ship put in to port until the weather cleared — which it eventually did —

But even with bright sunshine and a stiff breeze the trials of patience were not over — this particular wind being in a contrary quarter we began the maddening process of tacking about in an attempt to cheat it at a rate of one mile's headway for each three or four travelled — the whole contraption hopelessly inadequate —

Though soon even this was to seem purposeful compared with the calm that enveloped us — glassy water barely heaving — we lost headway till our gentle purling grew so quiet we might have been drifting backwards for all anyone could tell! — each day stretched longer than the last — the memory played tricks — the sea a mirage — within a week we forgot the dangers so recently survived and began to suffer that special boredom unique to travellers — the shipboard world being very small and amusements few — particularly for a closed household set apart from the rest by piousness —

Actually I have to admit to being visited by a wicked idea at this time which perhaps had some bearing on what happened — are you ready for ideas?

Far off course — out in that transparent universe — floating on the wide Atlantic above sunken mountains and valleys of sea monsters — with nothing the captain could do to turn the bow even a fraction of a degree — abandoned by the last gasp of breath and left helpless for eternity in a bubble of space — afloat on a soundless mirror where not a puff of air could reach us to nudge the sails —

In this era of steam you young people forget how difficult the old ways were with all the bother involved in mazes of rigging — and I suppose you've never thought of the sails themselves being especially heavy have you? well until I travelled neither had I —

Day after stifling day we drifted about in the tropics — our food stock dwindling — the fresh meat being finished we were down to dining on what a steward announced as "Salt junk with pickles if you please!" — we passed our time lounging in the shade of canvas awnings and only made shift to fan ourselves mechanically — the liveliest thing was a doleful periodic ringing of the bell which was occasionally done by a vastly handsome youth with wild fair hair — while Ann Whittaker complained that we should never have left Madeira —

Several others discussed in undertones the curiosity that among the four Gospel writers neither Mark nor John makes mention of the virgin birth — and I had my wicked thought (much as I later wished I could take it back!) — what proof was there — I thought — that the

virgin birth happened at all since God had never shown
the world another in more recent times (which He could
easily do) to have it verified scientifically?

At this moment the void around us was invaded by a
faint noise of galloping horses — the entire ship's company strained to hear — passengers peered in every direction for some explanation of this impossible thing —
horses — far out across the Atlantic Ocean! — indistinct
as they were at first they soon grew definite — there could
be no mistaking what we heard — yet the ship floated
steady — web of ropes silent — spars dark against a brilliant sky — hatches open as if the vessel itself gasped for
air while at all points of the compass the horizon presented
a ruled line as flat as that — distant bugles sounded *tara-
tara* and the thunder of hooves began to spread wider the
nearer it came — we looked around in mystification —
we looked up among the steeples of taut ropes — out
between curtains of slack sails — astern among capstans
and tackle — forward to where the bowsprit barely wavered — well! for a full twenty minutes those horses bore
down on us from nowhere and went galloping nowhere
until the din of their approach loomed tremendous and
you could hear hundreds of individual animals gasping —
riders shouted military oaths above a warm sea sluggish
enough for glue — there were witnesses because this was
heard by everyone gathered on the deck just as the baking
of bread could be smelt wafting out from the galley —

"Well I never!" said Ann crossly —

Big guns began to boom and invisible confusion took over with cavalry charging from opposite sides to swarm around us and converge above our heads — struggling and milling in every direction while we lolled on comfortable chairs and stared in amazement at the fascinating emptiness of a diamond hot sky where muskets apparently popped and soldiers apparently shouted like beasts only to be cut short by unbelievable blasts of nearby artillery — being answered with far-off grumbles from an enemy battery — and then in a lull came weird screams like the whistles of the Great Western Railway except that these came much faster and more terrifying as they whizzed past causing frenzy up there and stirring renewed outbursts of shouting and fresh bouts of musket fire —

You could say it was a kind of music — the way it came and went in rhythms broken by brief silences or swelled toward climaxes of confusion with sobbing choruses accompanied by whoops and snicks of bullets until finally the whole battle as a complicated symphony drifted away (making a good deal more sense than some of the pieces I heard at the Melbourne Philharmonic Society a few years back by the bye) — then the sun suddenly set and we sank trembling against the headrests of our deckchairs with no one daring to utter a word while the lurid and bloody splendour spread around us — we were filled with lingering horror of a sort hard to explain unless by recalling the single voice clearly heard to cry out "Keep going men — keep going whatever! — O God!" while

the tumult drifted further away toward the distant band
of sea which had already turned mauve where the rising
night stood as high in the sky as the water was deep in
that deepest ocean on earth — till the last horse snorted
and the last spur jingled and the last glimmer of dusk
faded — the Bengal lights were lighted while still we sat
as if we ourselves were prehistoric sea monsters caught in
a basket being pulled up by a net of cords —

Strange — beyond question stranger than the rickshaw
boy we saw later in Durban with buffalo horns growing
from his head or even the pagan woman who let herself
be burned alive on her husband's funeral pyre beside a
canal while the crowd of other ladies under umbrellas
pleaded with her not to weaken — and the meaning of
this battle in the air was plain to all but the most obsti-
nate —

There was a lesson in it — Beatrice told us "Our hopes
are destined to be marooned somewhere remote — untouched by the world's turmoil — somewhere de-
prived — " and she tottered away to her cabin —

With little else to think about during the aftermath
I entertained another of my wicked thoughts "What
if — " I whispered to the prophet who having stood rigid
beside me through the whole drama now bent down and
let a damp lock of hair brush my cheek "what if *you* were
to blame for this?" — he looked at me with such intense
interest I ached to make the point stick "So now I dare
say you will calm a storm if we run into one?"

I do hope in the next world to be spared meeting anyone the least like myself as I was in those days — but to be honest I can't believe I knew I was putting temptation his way — and despite his divine secret I didn't in the least believe he *was* to blame — yet shortly afterwards I had to live with my conscience because he was destined to face a most appalling storm at sea when maybe he thought he could control it and couldn't — then again in the matter of our awful tragedy perhaps he —

As for the rest — well the rest was little more than routine except that the delay meant we were running short of supplies as I say and had to put in at the nearest port — much to the relief of Beatrice Offley who felt dreadfully ill — even though she did find enough energy to dispute the idea that the invisible battle had been a sign heralding the Last Judgement — "With my training in the physical sciences" she said "I believe it was more likely an acoustical freak and a lingering remnant of the American War drifting in a lost pocket of air — they *were* American voices after all — "

The prophet didn't bother to hide how furious he was with her —

I believe she would have been glad that he so far forgave her secular opinion as to make no mention of this error of hers when giving her a decent burial at Ascension Island where we docked to refill our depleted water casks — yes she died poor thing — can you see us gathered round her grave while the captain read the service and my husband preached a sermon beginning "The House of the Dead is the place of birth"?

The mere thought of such a text makes me shudder now — with all I know —

The desolation of that island could hardly be imagined though the inhabitants began by welcoming us with wild demonstrations of jubilation and curiosity because they had not expected us to anchor any more than we ourselves expected it — but they shunned us when news got out of a death on board and a death which might be contagious.

The prophet called us his Household of Hidden Stars — being a secret order — the other eight members (surely I do not need to introduce myself into the picture?) — well you should place them in your mind on that stark and sweltering little island which is really no more than the one tropical mountain crag sticking up out of the Atlantic Ocean and adorned with big spiky plants — an island with a single harbour where miserable huts have been built of loose stone against a background blasted by the sun and grim enough to hope that neighbouring St Helena was as uncomfortable for the ogre Napoleon when he lodged there —

Imagine fifteen or twenty huts on a stony slope all but lost in a swirling cloud of seabirds so numerous you could not conceive how such thousands came to assemble at the one place or how they fed themselves or even found sufficient foot room to settle — the flurry of wings set the ribbons aflutter on Lady Edwina's bonnet as she stepped forward to drop a flower in —

The first of our burials and I wish with all my heart it had been the last!

Charlotte Smith was the dainty one who always put me in mind of celandines in mossy dells — the daughter of a mayor it was rumoured that she had shamed her father by an endearing native clumsiness — unlike clever Elizabeth Eyre who was her constant companion and took her hand at this crude graveside — indeed Elizabeth was forever taking Charlotte's hand and holding it too long — but I wouldn't have you think Charlotte was uncomplicated indeed she could be a conniver — and as a coward expert at having herself included at the centre of every plot — the necessary confidante to every meanness — we cannot all be perfect —

Now let's think who was standing next to them — Martha I believe — well Martha Sparrow used to puzzle me because she nourished some sadness which no amount of coaxing would induce her to confess not even to Hester Partington (if one credits Hester's word) who was perhaps the only truly wicked member of the sisterhood and therefore a person in front of whom things could be let slip with less than usual risk to the soul —

Flora Gilchrist stood to their right I recall — as ever habitually setting herself a little apart — she had been seven years old before she began to talk and the consequence throughout the rest of her life was an awkward disinclination to make friends — her father was quite a famous botanist I believe and so was her grandfather — indeed the grandfather had been the scientist who proved that forest trees attract rain (well I agree one would not think so right here and now with our drought!) but there must have been something in it because the government actually passed a law — don't ask me when — long before my day — to grow forests in Tobago for the sake of improving the climate — last century sometime — and she repeatedly boasted about one of her father's students who brought in the law to protect birds in Tasmania — a lovely idea — oh about thirty years ago — so much for Flora —

The fidgeting person was Lavinia Dudgeon — marvellous that a doctor at the asylum where she had been confined recognized her for a saint and not a lunatic at all —

Lastly my special friend Ann — dear tenderhearted Ann — almost a mother to me — author of the needlework you see on the wall here — no not that sampler this big piece which in case you are wondering is a chart of the more gruesome prophecies in Daniel and Revelation as they have come to pass in modern times with a great space left at the head of the design for the Advent.

What's that you say? Yes you are quite right you would remember another Elizabeth — Elizabeth Canning — she joined us in Melbourne as the daughter of an Australian merchant who lacked the refinement to know what to do with his money — especially since she had the lower half of her body missing altogether so she could not be expected to need a dowry — yes Elizabeth Canning became a favourite with us all.

The wind on that beastly island! and the birds! birds whirled and hurtled among us as if we were caught in a storm of big tropical flowers while we filled the grave with clattering stones and set up a cross — *Beatrice Ellen Offley* burnt into the wood — *R.I.P. In the bosom of the Lord* — then the prophet turned away and led us down the hill again —

Not till we reached the wharf did he declare his belief that Beatrice died in misery because she doubted we had been granted a premonition of the Last Judgement out there at sea — he confessed to taking the guilt of it upon himself for failing to bring her back to the faith in her last hours so he swore from that moment to bury the name he had been christened with — bury it as we buried her — "For a penance" he vowed "I shall become a new person so from now on you must call me Muley Moloch after the infamous Irish apostate and I shall bear the sins of the real Muley Moloch until I raise him from ignorance wherever he might be and save his soul despite himself — in return for the loss of Beatrice" —

So our prophet became Muley Moloch — we were astounded as you may imagine and I had a wicked revulsion against becoming Mrs Moloch but I dared not interrupt him while he was inspired — he promised that the electric lamps illuminating Buckingham Palace for the marriage of the Prince of Wales would one day be seen throughout London and would light the streets of every city on earth even in the colonies — that a misguided American lady would soon pretend to offer a key to the Scriptures all her own — that there would shortly be a showdown between Germany and France (which did break out as we know) also that Germany would win (which Germany did) — oh and he prophesied other things I have forgotten — no doubt they came to pass —

For a whole day after the burial a guilty constraint fell on us while we remained at Ascension Island — we ought not to abandon Beatrice — I was nagged by a suspicion that she expected us to live there for the remainder of our lives but as Flora Gilchrist said "The deed is done" — they ferried us out to the ship — we clambered aboard as it weighed anchor — almost immediately a brisk wind set the timbers creaking and squealing and rumbling and altogether sounding like a factory afloat while waves flew past dancing in sunlight —

All Beatrice's possessions and clothes were bundled up and cast into the sea —

I might say the captain made no end of fuss about changing our names on his manifest — arguing that it conduced to illegalities — but relented in the end and when we landed at Melbourne we stepped ashore as Mr and Mrs Muley Moloch and party.

How did I come to meet a prophet in the first instance? well to answer that one must delve right back into history

to the way I was before we met — a capricious girl of
fourteen — I still think of her as my true self — at that
time I had a friend (actually this was a cousin whom I
did not come to know earlier because her family was poorer
than ours and lived eight miles away) — this friend came
to stay and slept in my room and then I was allowed to
visit her house for a week and sleep in her room which
was above the farmhouse kitchen so that each morning
we woke to a sound of clanged pans and water tinkling
in the yard and the air full of bacon frying while we
turned on our narrow beds to look at each other across
the room — we fell in love you might say in the innocent
way of young girls so we could not bear being parted —
even when we got up we would stand side by side with
our arms on the same window ledge peering down across
a wall at the muddy drive and the duckpond beyond to
guess what the weather would be like for us — we confessed our separate plans of marrying remarkable men —

We saw ourselves — poor hopeless copy-cats that we
were — as brides completely bound by our husbands'
fortunes just as we would be liberated by their talents
and money because they were always to be respectably
ambitious — my cousin's name was Dora —

Her father called her Theodora and I might describe
him as a man who resented how niggardly God's gifts
had been in the matter of good looks while (as he complained) over-endowing him with intelligence of course
and then failing to put suitable opportunities his way —

Uncle Herbert his name was — an unwilling farmer just as his beasts were unwilling beasts and his crops unwilling crops — he was even an unwilling uncle to me — but this made no dint in the fact that I adored his damp farmhouse and cold stone kitchen and adored his meek silly wife and wished she could be my own mother and envied him his chickens which I walked among while throwing grain for them though I danced on the spot in terror of being pecked — the excitement of finding warm eggs buried in the straw nests was something I shall never forget — any more than wandering through barley with the tassels of it brushing my legs or Dora and me making ourselves sick eating elderberries — where was I?

Unwilling — yes.

My father would squeeze up his face while he commented that needless to say the farm was not Herbert's own and that Herbert merely rented it from a family called the Honeywoods — so the more I grew to love Dora the more I became aware of how shameful it was that her father had let his family down by owning no property because my father (even though a clergyman and everybody knew how poorly clergymen were paid for God's work) had amassed quite a comfortable little fortune through thrift and a good head for figures.

Judge Honeywood lived in the mansion called the Hall — Dora's farm was attached to the Hall — as indeed was the whole village of Cold Dean which it seems the judge took tremendous pride in (despite a rumour that the Coney family wanted to murder him) because all the villagers said he kept the closest eye on their affairs even to the thrill of privately dishing out alms to people in need and the thrill of privately punishing those who deserved punishment — he insisted on being godfather to every male child born there — and insisted his daughter should entertain the cottagers' children once a year at a Christmas party — what's more this party was not held in the servants' quarters (perish the thought of such missed opportunities for showing them their place) he would order the great front doors flung open so they could be led in through his hall among all its treasures to take high tea in his dining-room properly waited upon by his footmen in livery and received by his daughter precisely as if they were duchesses and ambassadors —

I'm telling you this because I once went with Dora and was fool enough to feel proud when an old footman with two silver pots leaned over me to ask "India or China madam?" and I promptly said "China" because he didn't know that China was my favourite country or that marriage to a missionary was among the adventures I entertained while lying in bed with a square of moonlight falling on my face as I gazed at the ceiling confessing to Dora my plans for my husband to convert the heathen if he were handsome enough — or that I had already begun collecting Chinese things such as the tiny silk painting of a coolie given me by another uncle and a packet of paper seeds which would open out to flowers if placed in a bowl of water — I never did place them in water because then I could never have them back as seeds though I was perfectly content with my faith that they *would* open if I chose to put them to the test —

All my life I have been an adept where faith is concerned —

The footman smiling gravely poured me this pale yellow tea from the full pot and then went on down the table asking "India or China sir? India or China madam? India or China sir?" and without waiting for answers poured them all tea from the other pot so I felt important until I tasted the vile stuff and knew I was honour-bound to drink it —

This was what privilege amounted to.

How did we get involved in such an old story? oh yes because of what happened later when my father cut all contact with Uncle Herbert and refused me permission to see Dora even to the point of repacking a little birthday present she had sent me and posting it back despite my howls of rage and grief or perhaps *because of* my howls of rage and grief but he never did explain and the only way I ever saw Dora from then on was through Judge Honeywood's daughter —

How to do justice to Miss Honeywood? — well she had spent the best years of her life perfecting the bright manner of someone who would never marry — she was dedicated to being a good sport and a cheerful breeze around her father's house in which there was nothing that was not precious and very little that was not fragile — she was the one you always saw (indeed at that stage I had never even had a glimpse of the old man) she made the cottagers' children feel — as she put it — *at home* and organized party games in the ballroom where she told everybody who had shoes to take them off — and she was the one to care for their spiritual wellbeing throughout the rest of the year by presiding over a private Sunday school class every second Sunday in the small drawing-room —

Dora and I were her helpers being of gentle birth and she treated us as little nieces to be bossed about in a way she never bossed the others — besides keeping us back for a quiet chat over a piece of cake when they trooped home to the market square with their catechism still to learn — I loved the cosiness of this time spent sipping Indian tea and shaking our heads over the vulgarity of the uneducated while waiting for my father's curate to call as he now did to preserve me from having to stay at the farm — the point being that despite Uncle Herbert my father valued his contact with the Honeywoods through me because they were people with such lovely manners as well as being rich — well on one occasion Miss Honeywood suggested we carry our refreshments into the garden and when she returned indoors to call some-body to find her shady bonnet (leaving us alone) Dora became suddenly agitated to my astonishment and strug-

gled with what appeared to be an attack of dumbness —
remaining dumb for the several precious minutes we had
together which was not like Dora — nor was it like Dora
to blush and twist her fingers in a knot —

She never got to the point —

So the months passed and we tried to remain as close
as ever but something had come between us and I believed
it to be my father's insult to her father so I told her I was
all burning up with hatred for that man (my father) which
was a daring thing in those days and almost as terrible
as blaspheming against God — yet even this fell short of
the desired effect and we never recaptured our closeness
until one Sunday she met me as we walked in the side
door of the Hall ushering the freshly scrubbed children
before us and took my hand on impulse carrying it up to
her lips — "Now you will see!" she whispered — you
may imagine how I trembled with excitement — well
what I was to see was nothing more exotic than a preacher
brought in by Miss Honeywood to inspire the village
urchins with an enthusiasm for God's work and I was
only struck by the queer fact that he spoke to the children
in their own rough language which he had mastered perfectly — and that his eyes were such a deep violet as to
be almost black —

The very next fortnight Miss Honeywood greeted me
with a shake of her perfect head and murmured "The less
said about poor Theodora the better perhaps because after
all no one can pretend it was altogether her fault" — I

was agog! — so after suffering the adoration of those little ogres with their grimy fingernails and after swallowing the lumps of cake I was privileged to share with Miss Honeywood I clanged my cup in its frail precious saucer — I invented a few excuses and rushed out — across the road I ran hoping to reach the farmhouse before our curate came bowling down the lane in the ancient brougham he used on his rounds of the parish —

I hurried in through the little old stone gateposts and down the drive to the farm not caring a fig about my new button shoes nor my bonnet being tugged by the wind and pushed back off my head to dangle behind me where it flopped about — until I caught sight of the low stone house jolting there before my blurry eyes and I stopped to get some breath back because the scene was just the same as ever —

Yet it wasn't the same — the dogs had gone and the ducks and chickens too — a couple of thrushes trilled in the deathly silence and then the single bell of a distant church began donging and the hollowness measured an immense silence to call up the saddest feelings which seemed to stretch back to a time before I had any memories at all —

I pictured myself hammering at the door and calling out or weeping and rushing round the back and I pictured myself throwing gravel up against the pane of "our" bedroom window or pushing open the iron gate and taking myself off to mope beside the duckpond or kick my heels in the kitchen garden or run through the fields beyond but I did none of this because I knew nobody was home — I knew it by the coldness on my skin — also that nothing could be done —

Once you start submitting to fate there's no end to it — I truly believe this was when my stoicism began — a stoicism that led to a life of humiliations — what I did was to set my bonnet straight and turn away with a vow to put all the happiness of that place behind me while I concentrated on walking like a young lady and concocting a good excuse for my emergence from the wrong gate — together with an excuse for the agitation which must show when I came to climb into the brougham and confront the curate's inquisitorial gaze.

Curates are without doubt the most hateful species in creation — but why on earth am I telling you this old stuff? excuse me —

Coughing.

What were you asking? ah yes of course I promised to get to the question of noises in the night didn't I? though you may rest assured on the issue of occasional screams at any time during the past thirty years that this may be simply part of our religious practice —

My father used to be very much attached to such comforts of his vocation as afternoon teas — with endless opportunities for airing the right opinions and harvesting agreeable little tiffs and even more agreeable little reconciliations to be concluded with a homily in support of his

acknowledged superiority in matters of the conscience —
do you think they ever grew tired of his overbearing
attentiveness? not a bit of it! they pressed him to come
back as soon as possible — so his life passed in a turmoil
of arbitrations before it was time for port after supper —

However where I was concerned — and this goes for
my mother and my sister as well — the truth was that
my timid sentimental father became a tyrant at the least
upset to his routine so when I was fifteen and taken by
Miss Honeywood to hear her visiting preacher deliver a
sermon at the chapel in town (how was she to know about
my father's lifelong abhorrence of chapel?) I was more
excited by the combined thrill of doing wrong and maybe
finding out what Dora meant when she had whispered
"*Now* you will see!" than by the visiting celebrity's brash
manner —

Not until I was in there and trapped in a pew by a
wave of shyness did the full force of my disobedience come
home to me — together with the profound disappointment of no one handsome having sat beside us and nothing
scandalous having so far happened —

The chapel was startlingly different from our lovely
dim old church — instead of carved stone and worn pav-
ing this stark room had plain whitewashed walls and a
crude silver cross on a table which had been spread with
a cloth too small and the wrong shape for it — even the
faces of the congregation appeared scrubbed clean of
expression — they stood up sat down knelt down and

stood again like a regiment that knows its drill — they sang their hymns in sober voices and seemed not at all to mind the predictable harmonies — such a contrast to the unearthly boy sopranos in the church choir — the service itself was as dressed-down and doggedly plain as the congregation — so Miss Honeywood with her embroidered bodice and her shrill confident inaccurate singing became so very noticeable I had to repress my pride in her — and I must say she behaved most handsomely during the sermon letting out appreciative Ahs and surprised Ohs when he said things like "Your souls are diseased — or rather dead — dead in sin — so now I am calling on you to wake up — be born again — arise from the dead for Christ to give you light" — that sort of thing — I know it so well —

In the end this sermon in fact made a notable impression on us all though at first my mind was repeatedly elsewhere —

I could not have been less interested in the preacher — his ears stuck out and his neck was not firm enough to fill the collar he wore so I entirely missed the text on which he based what he had to say — missed the part when no doubt he laid in the first broad strokes of his accusations against our sloth and corruption — but as he got wound up he broke through my indifference so that I grew to relish my strangeness in that place — I enjoyed feeling superior to the young organist who sat at his keyboard gazing raptly at the cluster of ridiculous pipes

painted pale blue with the most laughable gilt rims and
fipples (a hopeless player I might add as well as a hopelessly insignificant male with his spindly fingers) — the
preacher said "No free society ever existed without free
women" which arrested my attention — and I was further
alerted by hearing a curious reedy richness enter his voice
as he went on "Because morals are the work of women!"
I looked up to find him gazing at me — I was doubly
astonished — "Women are always the first to heed the
word of the Lord — so you ladies are our strength and I
want you to know we need you in this place — we weak
men — you have already seized the privilege of freedom
and the humble evidence is that you were able to decide
to come to this service today — a freedom to be treasured
because in other parts of the world you would be pre-
vented — in Catholic countries young women are less
mistresses of their actions than in England — even during
these wicked times!"

That naked room took on a new character because now
I saw details which were to remain in mind as pegs on
which I could secure the sentiments I most wished to
remember — at the same time I suddenly found myself
annoyed by all the coughing and shuffling going on
around me —

A shaft of light fell aslant a wall where I studied the
text painted above the vestry door — *He that hath ears to
hear let him hear* — while I grappled with the strangeness
of the idea that it might have read "She that hath ears"
and "Let her hear" — the preacher went on "The virtue

of women secures order throughout our whole nation" —
I stared at a brass candelabrum hanging by a chain far
thicker than necessary — his argument branched out in
a new direction "As there was a beginning so there will
be an end — because the very idea of Being depends upon
an end to it — without an end there is no proof of a
beginning and therefore to deny the end is to deny the
beginning and to blaspheme against God's word in the
Book of Genesis!" — stared at the hymn numbers displayed like Egyptian designs in their little bracket as his
voice rang out even more compellingly "By no means
does the end destroy the value of life — what is precious
is only precious because it can be lost — and *will* be lost!
Friends — the end will soon be among you and for this
you should give thanks to the Almighty — it is not because death will bring an end to my tribulations that I
give thanks but because death will bring my joys to an
end — my faith to an end — my riches my happiness to
an end — this — this is why we must avoid sin — because the end of sin can only give meaning to sin and you
need to strain every sinew of the soul in denying sin the
least hold on your life — therefore keep alert!" — by now
all shuffling had ceased — the congregation listened with
an unaffected piety — "Sin will creep in by whatever
means the Devil can find" he continued "even food may
become evil if we are tempted to find it tasty — lots of
sneaking tricks — and those sins we have not avoided we
shall need to root out in a hurry before the end is upon
us" (a lady cried aloud for mercy) "before Jesus walks the

earth once more — because you may be sure He will come as simple and pure as a flame" (she cried out again) "He wishes to find us burning with faith and eager for the moment when everything and everyone we hold dear is struck away and destroyed!" these words flashed like lightning in the hush — he seemed about to add more but thought the better of it —

I noticed he looked drunk when he left the platform uncertain of where to place his feet — eyes huge and shining — then a chapel elder twice his age bowed before addressing him in a croak as "Our blessed Father in Israel" —

Afterwards we took refreshments in the vestry and the preacher continued to fascinate me though he appeared much smaller than in the pulpit — back to the way he had been at the Hall — all the more disturbing then that people were now calling him a prophet — Sister Briscoe took his arm "The Lord visited us indeed" she murmured —

I was flattered when he remembered me and took a few moments to ask after my health before coming out with something commonplace and neutral "The times call for uncommon deeds!" as he turned to devote himself wholly to Miss Honeywood's complaint against Jesus' preference for Charity over Faith and Hope — "Um — Um — " he contributed while vigorously nodding though Miss Honeywood scarcely noticed because she never expected anything other than acquiescence — an amazing tingle fluttered in my throat — I was alert with astonish-

ment — my instincts told me it was for *me* that he kept
her there — for me that he proceeded to consult her not
only on such topics as peacock butterflies but oddities
like the correct number of waistcoat buttons gentlemen
leave unfastened when seated as distinct from when they
stand —

By this time everyone else had given away vying for
the least particle of his interest and of course they themselves were aware of the honour of having the great lady
come all the way to town to join them at chapel —
especially as she had previously been known to favour the
highest church practices —

Even then I wanted to laugh at those primpers rinsing
their nonconformist cups and dusting crumbs from the
table — my sense of fun had not yet been put to the
torture — I wanted to laugh at the ushers straightening
chairs and beginning to bolt the doors so even the judge's
daughter shot a look at the blessed clock and said "Is *that*
the time!" as she smoothed her gloves to a satisfaction
over each elegant finger and then in an abstracted mood
stretched out the whole arrangement palms up — then
backs up — "Now come along Catherine" she bullied me
affectionately "say thank you for the inspiring sermon and
lead the way" — however we had scarcely passed under
the iron arch of the outside gate than the preacher appeared
at the door calling "Oh I say Miss Byrne excuse me" so
I glanced up and caught his ecstatic expression and left
my protector — drifted back again among those flurries
of dust perpetually patrolling the footpaths of Stroud —

In a trance I climbed the stone steps — delayed briefly when my skirt caught on a rosebush and I stopped to free myself — accidentally pricking my finger and tugging the glove off to protect it from being stained with a blood spot —

I recollect to this very day hesitating on the threshold to lick my finger (too innocent for understanding omens) while he invited me in with the explanation that he had a text for me and that Miss Honeywood had left her hymnal behind too.

Do you know Gloucestershire? well someday you will I am sure — beautiful Gloucestershire.

He was standing in the dim room between the lectern and a table covered with a thick cloth (I can still see a fringe of little pom-poms) — and then right there in front of me he began to rise up — glossy pumps lifting clean off the carpet until I could have passed my hand under them while he gazed down at me from a brilliant face full of features!

Thirty-two years ago — and all this while his miracle has been kept a secret between us! — but of course I may be wasting it on you — you may think flying nothing so very special.

When it comes to the point I suppose *I* didn't know what to make of it so I just went along with things as usual and expected that even this would end in disappointment.

*   *   *

You will call me hopeless of course there is no getting away from that but I was haunted by what I had witnessed —

It was odd enough to be sure (I beg your pardon? no matter) because not only were the visiting preacher's shoes rising off the carpet but he — and he had struck me as stern during his harangue in chapel — he came alive with laughter "Hope!" he cried in an adolescent voice despite his twenty-eight years "Hope is the greatest of the three!" rustling towards me inside his hot suit like a bird —

I dared not meet his challenge or watch his floating feet so I stared to one side at a framed etching of a lamb hung up by a belt around its middle — well that was the moment when I knew this business of flying was not quite decent and would need to be kept secret from the world —

My whole story is a catalogue of secrets if you like —

One thing led to another and the young preacher was invited back to the Hall but that week the Sunday School had to be cancelled owing to Miss Honeywood's headache — you may imagine my discomfort with a whole hour to kill — until the obliging fellow volunteered to walk me in the garden where he soon confessed that he hoped to live a private life of secrets too huge for telling — I was captivated — we strolled — engrossed in profitable conversation — I had never felt such happiness — we listened to bees hum around the dusty perfume of lavender bushes — he boasted modestly about his father having died Warden of the Worshipful Company of Cordwainers which is to say bootmakers — I couldn't think of a boast about mine — meanwhile his father had passed on the whole art — mine had passed on nothing but rules for table manners — his father had taught him everything from how to soak tannin out of oak bark to how to stitch flat seams around a welt — I was speechless and all the more speechless when the preacher dropped to his knees — surprise upon surprise he grasped my foot which he placed in his lap to show his skill at fitting customers by the feel of their toes through the uppers (this was when he discovered I had a toe missing) while advising them on the superiority of local Stroud products over the finest imported leathers from Cordova — carried away by enthusiasm he promised to show me his realm in all its manifold prospects — beginning with a tannery — an offer which struck me dumb —

Naturally my moment of silence was interpreted — there have been many such moments for which I have had to pay during the rest of my life.

Funny you should ask because in fact he did suggest a visit to the abattoirs as well if I wished to appreciate the true provenance of shoes — such shoes as I had worn until then all unwittingly — what a prospect! — I recall fumbling for the handkerchief in my sleeve and pressing it against my nose while the garden brightened and the perfumed skies went to my head —

I declined —

But I never could resist the thrill of adventure for long and I suppose I fully intended to visit this new world of the tannery plus any number of abattoirs as well for that matter even though he warned me they were beyond doubt "grisly" — if only I could concoct a clever enough strategem to keep my father from knowing — yet the lure of the thing lay in the power it gave me to let loose a tornado of parental fury if I chose — just think of the crimes I was accumulating — an interview with a chapel man including a private conversation in Judge Honeywood's small drawing-room and a walk around the garden during which I had let him kneel to take my foot in his lap while he corrupted my virgin fancy with horrifying visions of flayed carcases and of skins being salted while the meat was lugged away for carving into the separate categories of delicacy and offal.

Can't you just picture my father making ready to kill me? — his neck swelling purple inside a tight collar and his bald head starting with perspiration (dear Reverend Byrne!) he was so very English —

Come to think of it everything we suffer as colonialists in Australia might be because we are from England and this land doesn't like the smell of us — do you feel it? — but no — how would you?

Back home people carry off their hypocrisy with unbeatable grace — which I regret to say you local types have never mastered — and the secret of this grace is an

Englishman's tact — by the bye allow me to warn you against confusing hypocrisy with tact — what could be more different than a person who pretends to be what he isn't and a person who knows when and how to respond out of consideration for others?

Come to think of it maybe the reason I could never please my father was because I had no tact — I could never tell when or how to respond —

Yet England used to be a happy place for a growing child and I feel sorry for anybody without the sort of recollections I have — scuffing through drifts of fallen beech leaves in autumn to churn them up and kick yellow cascades in the air — lying down among them if it wasn't raining — gazing at the sky through new bare branches —

Glorious!

As a child I was a wild thing who had been trapped and apparently tamed — a child not often praised and then generally when I stayed out of the way or when I showed a talent for obedience or when I kept my pinafore clean while playing out of doors or when I did well at elocution or practising scales but never for my lively mind or my pluck — I decided I liked everything about my new friend the preacher except the warts on his hand which could be felt pressing on my fingers as he first took me into the dark by which I mean not only the dark of superstitions but his actual world —

He had no idea his darkness was dark at all so he offered

it to me quite as a favour and explained that in the interests of the maturity which would be required of me by his imminent fame I ought not to pass up the opportunity of watching him at his humble craft (you see how little his insight helped him foretell his own future?) — and a pair of shoes he had promised to make for Judge Honeywood would provide the means because they were to be of the finest box calf so he would have to attend to every detail beginning with the choice of leather —

Meanwhile events moved faster than I knew — at least between him and the Honeywoods —

I suppose what gave Miss Honeywood such a nose for matrimony was not being married herself — and for a similar reason I found myself in some sense ashamed of the preacher's peculiar powers now I suspected I would marry him —

The first I knew of a change was the frightful scene between my father and the curate who was supposed to have monitored what I did when I went to the Hall — though the poor horrid creature had nothing but guess-work to go on and was left with very little option in the matter really since his duties were simply to set me down and then pick me up eighty minutes later — culminating in the fellow's dismissal and our immediate departure dressed in our very smartest clothes bound for the Hall which we had never before visited as a family —

You must picture us arriving and being intimidated by Miss Honeywood's cordiality as she conducted us across

the hall to the large drawing-room — a splendid blue
and white affair with huge chandeliers and floor-to-ceiling
windows from which velvet curtains were drawn aside to
open upon a view of the garden — while gilded chairs
kept sentry duty either side of the doorways in a manner
forbidding to anyone tempted to sit on them — I remember some delicate tables placed under the mirrors
too — yes yes and a pale blue carpet lying like an im-
maculate patch of sky separating us from a double door
at the far end of the chamber — you would never find
anything to equal it in the colonies — the carpet was of
such soft luxurious stuff that everywhere you trod your
footprints remained clearly marked —

For once I had the advantage of my father — being a
familiar in the house and the one whom the footman
smiled at —

While we assembled there suitably diminished by the
setting I found myself fascinated by that chaos of ghostly
shoe-prints trampling round in a bewildered patch —
then the two halves of the door swung open to reveal an
astonishing little man wearing a powdered Captain Cook
wig as became gentlemen of the old school — he had
knee-breeches with buckle shoes and was already shuffling
towards us on bandy legs.

God must be like this — limping across the sky —
twisted by age and frail from his burden of sifting the
world's dross for each rare grain of truth —

I had never before seen such an ancient specimen —

he wore lace at his cuffs and collar with the air of someone
hastily dressed — but there could be no doubting who
he was though it suddenly struck me as funny that he
should be spoken of in hushed tones and sent messages
of gratitude — even by his own daughter —

His lean face folded in on itself to shape a permanent
smile which surely must have mystified the criminals he
despatched to the mercies of Bridewell (such a name for
a prison!) — my blood stopped at the sight — he stepped
out of the last century with that peculiar grandeur which
seems to our modern taste next door to obsequious —
watching us shrink as he dragged one foot and primly
placed the other like a marionette —

He babbled greetings — toothless gums slapping together wetly — as he waved an arm behind him to beckon
somebody forward — then who should I see letting the
weighty drapes of the portière swish closed as he emerged
from the private chamber — draining me of blood while
at the same time pumping my heart with cold air and
then hot air — who but my very own preacher? —

The palpitations grew worse until the room became a
bellows — by turns pressing me down and puffing me
up —

Judge Honeywood proceeded to behave for all the world
like somebody ordinary — introducing the preacher to
my horrified father my mother my sister and to his other
guests that day — a neighbour called Major McDonald
and the solicitor Weedham's widow who later gave it as

her opinion that one knew enough about the poor fanatical young man's family just by their ugly name —

Do you wonder if it makes me shiver to think back on this and face the fact that it was not a scene in something tastefully hilarious by Arthur Sullivan? — well I stood like an idiot and gaped — I who was supposed to be so famous at showing nothing and keeping secrets!

The judge piped up and promised us a "special treat" as he put it while his little white eyebrows wiggled independently "this being a remarkable fellow and a remarkable occasion all things considered" — or something of the kind — then to my amazement actually took my father by the sleeve bringing him face to face with the preacher — as close as this — and pronounced the engagement "a remarkable match" brightly offering us all glasses of hock — including me.

The Honeywoods were one of three wealthy families in the district — squires on a grand scale and notable throughout the county — as well as owners of the best living for a parson —

"Yourself being a man of the cloth and all that" the judge continued with his voice sugared by the wine — all the while tweaking my father's sleeve "you will not thank me if I offer you moral advice I dare say and I'm sorry for it with all my heart as I am sorry you will not need reminding that if there is one thing more delightful than memories of having raised a fine girl tis I am sure the gratification of passing her future into the care of another" — but if he noticed Miss Honeywood wince he did not hesitate —

Habitually quickwitted thanks to his suspicious nature my father soon saw what matters were afoot without his knowledge (without my own either I might add!) — but I'm sure he never guessed that my mind filled with a single thought which was not "Am I really to marry?" but "Shall I really escape?" — and although I felt a tremor of happiness please do not imagine I had planned to marry anybody yet — let alone a common bootmaker —

"Nowadays soft kid is as rare as salvation!" the judge prattled on —

My father prepared to explode — not least because his suspicions must have tweaked him now we could see that both cobbler and patron suffered the selfsame limp which gave them an appearance of conspirators in some mockery of the Creator's work — but people who prepare to explode seldom do do they? —

The judge invited us to cast a more exact eye over the cut of the shoes while his voice trembled as he explained "So you see why I am all the more to be thanked for agreeing to let the fellow go" — go *where?* I wanted to shriek because this was all too appalling and too great a relief — then I remembered having confessed my Chinese ambition to Miss Honeywood! — but how could I deny that mad fancy at this stage — good heavens I had only chosen China as my favourite because the very word filled me full of fear — like the word "missionary"!

I suppose I expected somebody to comment on my betrothal if that's what it was or at least say Oh my goodness gracious what a *wild* girl (which might have given me an excuse to slip out of the arrangement) but instead they looked at me as though I was doing something I had always done and would never grow out of —

My father was on the brink of bursting with rage at any minute but in the event he showed none of the courage he threw around so recklessly when the butt of his anger was only my mother or me and took the easy way out — I dare say he lives with the disappointment of having missed his opportunity —

And any anticipated disgrace to our name must surely have paled beside the reality of me managing my skirts up on the roof here a couple of months ago with nails clenched between my lips and hammer in hand pounding away in an effort to repair a leaky slab of bark before the oncoming storm — can you imagine!

I was sure to have made a mess of things even if I had been wooed by a regular dullard in the expected manner — so I probably did the best thing given the circumstances — and then Judge Honeywood led us outdoors to present us with a wedding gift — the very latest foible — a lawn-mowing machine of the kind tried out by the Queen herself.

My full name is Catherine Jane — née Byrne — I was born on the tenth of March 1850 at five-and-twenty to two in the morning at home in Stroud so you may deduce my present age for yourself now there is apparently no such nicety as concealment left me at forty-eight — and I wish I could be sure that I am a good person — but what I can say is that I am a person who has quite given up the vanity of expecting to get away with anything —

That may be to do with being a Byrne — because when I think of my family I cannot believe in myself — Byrne is supposed to be a Catholic name and yet we never had the least taint so far as I ever heard — even Catherine creates doubts because one has to deny being Katherine with "K" or Catharine with "ar" or whatnot —

I think I ought have been christened Alice and that our family ought to have been Middletons — I am convinced that Alice Middleton could nowise have become engaged to anyone so hastily — the shock hit me twenty-four hours later — I knew I had to escape him or that together we had to escape respectable society —

This idea continued to seethe in my head when I plunged into working with him on his ministry — finding I could be useful because I knew so many of the county identities besides knowing (from my father's table conversation) their chief frailties —

A week later Flora Gilchrist chanced along —

Flora had the advantage of being grown up and able to do anything she wished — maybe she could persuade him to marry her instead? — but no — only later did I realize she was to be the first of many trials I must undergo for the sake of keeping my faith — and oh how I envied her because she knew how to flatter him and improve his arrangements without treading on Miss Honeywood's corns as his patroness and yet be safe from his advances — I envied her also because she proved she could speak his language when she said "Life is an unexplored country the wonder and beauty of which calls to me every hour of every day."

This was at a time when I had to face the embarrassment of his visits for dinner — my family staring in complacent disbelief while he toyed with cutlery he had never been taught to hold correctly — he chewed with his mouth open and every so often ducked his head down to the plate — not to mention his habit of licking his knife and fork clean when he had finished or replacing them on the cloth exactly as he had found them before he began to eat — or gulping Mother's pudding or guzzling Father's port — until the household buzzed with a general air of justice being seen to be done —

I made a virtue of not showing how ill I felt — the same when he perched on the sofa and picked at his fingernails or primly set his hat on his exasperating head while indoors and still with the ordeal before him of having to kiss my mother's hand — besides the outburst of titters he provoked by calling her "Mum" —

We had to endure the whole catalogue of niceties each time he was invited and although I gave him hints as to what was wrong he refused to listen — indeed the more

discreet the hints the more they galled him — and yet —
and yet he did offer me freedom and his unconventional
ideas did open whole worlds of bold new vistas —

Is it any wonder if I looked to the colonies as the best
solution once we were married? —

Curiously enough he was the one to give me my chance
of breaking our engagement "You can take yourself off
home to the parsonage" he growled one afternoon "because
I cannot carry you on my conscience" — "I shall not do
any such thing!" I retorted and this checked him —
"There's no comfort in my life" he explained quietly —
"Nor in mine" I replied — "Do you understand?" he
shouted — and I shouted back "No I do not!"

Then I added in a more ladylike manner "If I go home
to my father it will be because I have decided to go" —
"There's nothing more to say" he said and yet that night
I wept into my pillow and in an agony of mind silently
vowed not just to abandon him but to abandon religion —
I would leave him to Flora! — I went on raging like a
mad creature and only brought myself to reason by crawling out in the cold to kneel on the floor until I nodded
off halfway through my prayers —

It brings me up short to think of my casual tone when
eventually I came out with the suggestion that we escape
to the colonies and how serene I was in my ignorance of
the size and violence of the oceans one had to cross —
but do we learn? can even risking our lives teach us? —

It's the trivial things that catch us on the hop.

"Our mission" Flora agreed when my idea was put by
our leader as his own "will be purely and simply perfecting
ourselves."

I've told you about the voyage — us becalmed and
burying Beatrice Offley — well there were storms too and
days of misery belowdecks — so you may imagine what
we thought when we docked in Port Melbourne and drove
to the town after months of travel — supposedly at the
ends of the earth — only to find people exactly like the
people we had left behind at home! hundreds of comically
respectable idiots strolling around sunny streets in frock
coats and crinolines wishing each other "Good morning"
under the huge blank sky! —

I could have killed them!

That very year Melbourne was declared a city — proud
of its Botanical Garden and on the eve of greatness with
gold about to be discovered — indeed as we drove along
wide streets one might imagine we were in a real capi-
tal — all very dignified — provided one could ignore fre-
quent glimpses of the huddle of tin buildings tacked on
behind the columns and porticos — Mr Moloch appeared
enormously relieved but from my viewpoint it would not
do — nor would people plainly given to wild notions of
respectability as their right! —

Apparently I was fated to have no peace of mind in
Australia either unless we got away from the city's false
façades and the horrors lurking there (Melbourne being a
town where no sooner does a good clever man arrive than

he finds himself caught up in a public-house brawl and
has his skull cracked open by a pack of brutes) —

So soon as tickets could be arranged we took berths on
a small coastal packet and headed north seeking somewhere innocently primitive — the prophet blowing the
clarion and rallying his Household of Hidden Stars — we
sang "Onward Christian Soldiers" as we trooped aboard
eager to do battle on Christ's behalf —

Meanwhile at close quarters I had discovered that our
ladies were not so perfectly good as they had seemed in
England — I grant you their spite was a refined class of
spite and their coarseness seldom physical (being mainly
coarseness of sympathies) but spiteful and coarse they
were — and there's nothing like a voyage to bring things
to a head —

The little ship proved much less comfortable than the
big one thanks to the shock running through its whole
frame every time a paddle vane struck the water — thanks
to the soot forever raining on deck too — and thanks to
the cramped quarters — not to mention an added worry
that in place of an interminable ocean we were now presented with interminable unbroken woodlands stretching
the full length of the coastline — the Australian wilderness — with not a solitary sign of civilization for days on
end until we reached the whale butchery at Eden —

With the stench of Eden behind us we arrived in Yandilli at last.

You may think Yandilli all right but let me tell you

the port looked ridiculously rudimentary to us — indeed until we rounded the point we might never have guessed it was here at all — so when the packet tied up to a rickety pier very few other passengers got off with us (I am talking about a time before the days of the Illawarra and South Coast Shipping Company) and they soon disappeared along the shady lower level of a two tiered structure — we took deep breaths of wild air and waited to watch the boat depart without us — our last link with England — its paddles beginning to slap the water again — the deck visibly shuddering — tall funnel puffing black smoke — booms swinging over as the ugly little sails tugged taut — then I remember my husband suddenly becoming furtive and herding us along the wharf like the secret society we were — we left our baggage in a pile — trunks and suitcases stacked round the crate containing the lawn mower — because there was not a single porter in sight — only a couple of bystanders who lingered to look us over in so frank a manner as to risk actual rudeness — fragments of the picture remain painfully clear in my head — they stared at everything from our hemline to our bonnets while we climbed some damp steps to the upper level where an open-mouthed child watched us emerge into the light and clung to a man who crossed himself —

We were among Catholics!

Very moving it was — no I don't mean to sound sarcastic! — we were isolated by our faith in a place so bare that our message had never before seemed more beautiful or more fragile —

At one stage the district had been a single property but folk soon told us there was a curse on it thanks to that lady who murdered her husband — Governor Gipps had to send troops in — what was she called? — she ended up becoming the first gentlewoman hanged in New South Wales which provoked Mr Moloch to joke that he hoped in his case there would be safety in numbers! — setting Flora Gilchrist and the entire mission laughing at my expense —

This was the fifth of March 1868 — and the horror had taken a step closer — so had Louisa —

There's no doubt I found the jibe quietly upsetting but I would also have to say that to some extent I tend to feel more satisfied when I am quietly upset than at most other times —

Poor things — those people who built "Yandilli" — both of them — especially because many wives might contemplate murder without necessarily knowing how or even having any real intention of putting it to the test though I do not mean to implicate *myself* nevertheless I would suggest that murder may not seem so very out of the way if once we have the privilege of looking into the souls of quite ordinary folk —

By the bye I hope you do not mind our cats — actually they are Louisa's now — I've lost count.

Not a happy history — well I heard that the local

community sighed with relief when all but the logging camp at the south end of "Yandilli" property came to be pegged out by a surveyor — it was sold to us at auction just in time for some harebrain to discover gold in the creek — so we had to face the fact that within a week a thousand diggers might descend on us.

Was that your father who found the gold? I believe it was! but in the event there was not enough of it to stir any real interest —

The point is that when we compare truth with lies each item of the truth looks sadly simple beside the variety of lies one could possibly tell instead — comparing one's actual life and one's hopes for one's life is a little bit like that too.

What's that you say? how did we manage?

It was difficult because the prophet recruited gentle-women with ever more obvious disabilities — a missing ear a missing breast a missing nose — until in Melbourne he converted Elizabeth Canning who was on crutches — bravest of the brave Elizabeth put a strain on the rest of us not to help her or keep fussing around her when she seesawed along till eventually we procured the only wheel-chair in the district (you probably remember how you used to jump when you heard it rumble across the floor-boards?) — don't ask what Louisa is missing —

Once we settled at the mission we found ourselves spending more and more hours of each day being brought face to face with the most horrible realities and laying bare our tender hearts in order to clear out every taint — well — wickednesses and vanities — often enough I sit here with my eyes closed against the day blazing out there while I marvel at what we survived — such scrutiny and punishments — not to mention monstrous expectations —

All people live in fear of the afterlife no matter how great their faith and this applies especially to those of us who study the Scriptures and understand what a riddle the whole caboodle is — so no wonder we do our utmost to recognize signposts in this life to prepare us for the next — and why shouldn't there be equivalents for everything in Heaven just as humble habits reveal profound truths? —

So the voyage which began as a grand adventure ended in stagnation? — then this had to be faced up to — simple —

The idea of a *continuing* journey took hold though we had no idea how long a journey it might be nor how many wrong turnings we might take before tragedy caught up with us to bring us to our senses — as Christian says in *The Pilgrim's Progress* "things pleasant and dreadful go hand in hand" — which they did —

It has to be admitted that we were mainly happy in those days — singing to the sublime swish of brooms and clash of buckets because we knew we had been accepted as God's elect thanks to Mr Moloch who preached that "Woman is to redeem Man by becoming his second bride

which is to say his second Eve" — a text quite explicit
concerning his choice of spinsters as disciples — besides
being another riddle — for a while our days were filled
with hard work and merriment but soon the suspicions
began seeping back and once again we had to be vigi-
lant about our thoughts because otherwise things went
wrong — a back-door key mislaid — hens failing to produce eggs — the prophet himself suffering a bout of flat-
ulence — such problems multiplied and had to be
investigated —

Investigations became the centre of our routine —

There came a time when I was made to lie on the floor
in the shape of a cross for seven hours so that our mare
would not die of the foal she was struggling to produce —
then poor Lavinia who always had to hunt down whatever
word she needed bustled in all of a bother and announced "Kick — um — desperate — quick — no —
the heartbeat — what do you say? — thorn — thirst —
it's born — "

For the rest — well — after breakfast we laboured in
the field as the Bible exhorts us to do (or else in the house
like Dorcas if the weather was wild) each duty a joy so
that every small pain helped fortify us against the great
void — my main challenge was to keep up to the mark
and not fail to be worthy of the example set by the others
because one thing for sure is that Flora Gilchrist and Ann
and Martha and the rest (except Hester Partington) proved
themselves better souls by far than I and I envied them

the ease of their goodness while my goodness had to be squeezed out of me if I was to produce any at all.

What's that you say?

On the contrary I do not recall a single instance when Mr Moloch laid a finger on anybody either as punishment or encouragement because he kept a very proper distance and even during the fiercest beatings he was scrupulous about leaving it to us and never taking part other than to clarify the nature of our faults for others to judge and act upon —

True — while I lived from day to day it seemed a hard life with not enough joy for a fair share but now I look back on it I can see straight away that it was probably a good life — even though the punishments started very early in the piece — perhaps the best kind of life imaginable —

Our very first disciple — Flora Gilchrist — who had been a leading Stroud Methodist made it her special role to take up the least thing my new husband let fall and magnify it into a doctrine which she then policed with the utmost rigour —

Throughout our early years together she performed this duty — the moment any problem of faith arose Flora set to work on it like a crosscut saw working a deep cut when she applied her principles to it this way then cutting deeper by dragging the same deadly edge of righteousness the other way — again remorselessly and again — she had absolutely no sense of humour — so you may imagine

there was never much love lost between her and Lady
Edwina Wyntoun — the one who brought us enough
money just in time to fulfill our plan of sailing for Australia — but who was not accustomed to being ordered
about — especially when it came to the proprieties —

Before she fell ill Flora had been quite pretty in her
own way and proud of her golden curls — whereas Edwina who could never have been called pretty made a
point of her fine discrimination — I believe they both
thought me a ninny and I was one of the few subjects on
which they could reach agreement in a perfectly amiable
way —

Naturally I could not boast of the power I had over the
prophet although every decision he took began with a
suggestion from me — just tuck that away for future
reference (though you should remember that this influence was utterly without effect when it came to drawing
him close or to satisfying my needs or even to luring him
to take my hand for no other reason than to show me he
knew there was panic knocking at my heart) — I had the
unfair privilege of pretending to appear quite helpless and
of laughing off any hint he let slip in private by saying
You will make me split my sides with your suspicions
my dear I do declare I could never dream of any such
thing —

You see what we were like?

I have already confessed whose idea it was to flee England together and set sail for the colonies — I dare say

I deserve no sympathy if I complain that I spent a good deal of the voyage as my husband's secretary taking dictation while he was inspired to compose a book of rules for thwarting Baal and thirty-eight prohibitions necessary for reforming chapel worship — all the while the important thing was that I should protect him from guessing I was less ashamed of his illiteracy than his lack of manners.

As for the question of appearances — it is no use looking for evil in obvious places — Flora helped by criticizing my handwriting.

Yes for several years Yandilli did seem secluded and primitive enough — but then our privacy began to be blighted by nosey parkers and we became victims of gossip — with neighbours discussing Mr Moloch and myself (as husband and wife) speculating on when they might expect the first sign of fruit from our supposed labours — and taking it in bad part that we presented them with nothing —

I dare say even the sisterhood began to blame me for my apparent barrenness — and quite suddenly I found myself overwhelmed by a new desperation to hide somewhere even more remote — matters came to a head one morning when I went to the Yandilli shop to buy some haricot beans and sell some spinach — interrupting Mrs McNeil who had just said the whole world wondered at such a weedy chap being able to keep up with the many demands made on him! — of course this was unbearable especially as I was still untouched myself —

I pretended to have forgotten my list — as ladies we were condemned by our genteel upbringing and I dare say in my shoes the others would have blushed as painfully as I did — and I *did* despite being the only one of our Household with the least claim to know what carnal knowledge is —

I am glad to be making progress against the horrible habit we are taught of cushioning the truth for the sake of saving face —

I was so desperate to get away that the minute we heard of a suitably barbarous place being up for sale I nagged Mr Moloch to set off after the owner who had gone to the goldfields — "Very well" he said quietly "I intend following your advice but this will be a new beginning for us all and from now on you must no longer share my bed" he silenced my protests with a raised hand "it is God's will that you sleep alone — don't ask me to explain" —

He gave no reason and brooked no opposition — I leave you to imagine what state such sheer unfairness threw me in though I excused him by privately blaming my cough which must have been keeping him awake at night — and thus matters between us remained at sixes and sevens while my illness worsened until I was too disastrously weak to care anymore and collapsed on my lonely couch with a sigh of relief.

I am doing my best to explain the circumstances of the whole story as fast as I can — trying not to get it back to front —

I was so ill — the Lord's hand lay heavily upon me — He cut off every comfort at a blow — He smote me with a fever and a consumption and a guilty conscience — all but carrying me off — night after night I read about myself in the Book of Job "Terrors are turned upon me" you know the passage? "they pursue my soul as the wind — and my welfare passeth away as a cloud — and now my soul is poured out upon me — the days of my affliction have taken hold upon me — my bones are pierced — and so forth and so on — " I read it over and over "by the great force of my disease is my garment changed — it bindeth me about as the collar of my coat — "

If you ask me I caught the disease kissing Beatrice Offley to console her on her deathbed when no one else would touch her — I remember she whispered as we made ready to lower her into the pinnace for rowing ashore "There's nothing of me left to save" — then when I had comforted her she added "I have been hollowed out" she coughed "All that's left of me is my skin" and later as the oars fell to with a rhythm and we drew near the quay she added "Completely filled with foul disease" —

Odd that when my own crisis came I found I could face hidden truths about myself as if I had become a separate person appointed to the task of judging me —

for example being able to hear my father's accent in my own voice — and (when the evil Hester held a mirror for me) seeing a person with my grandmother's nose which I would never believe I inherited as well as Uncle Herbert's ineffectually villainous contraction of the eyebrows — all of which explained why I was left to suffer alone in my silent bed apart from fleeting visits by only the kindest and the cruellest of the Stars even though I lay on the verge of death —

In this condition I sought the Lord but He gave no answer — He afflicted me with helplessness — He scared and terrified me with dreams and brought down the night upon me at noon covering me with shame until I cried out "I am vile — I am afraid — help me!" only to have Hester's puffy lips smile into my face and open to ask "What did you say dear?" —

I no longer thought myself a whole person — just a thing which must breathe by fighting for each breath with skill and courage — the skill of securing enough air to survive until the next heartbeat but not so much as to provoke fits of coughing — the courage to try for another —

Incidentally people who regard coughing as a mild inconvenience do not know what they are talking about — some coughs shake your soul into bleeding fragments —

I punished myself with complete surrender to the illness until it struck me blind and dumb and I remained insensible for days with my eyelids so tightly closed they might have grown together and my mouth sealed on my tongue — so far was I deceived that I mistook this flowering of my illness and the severity of its climax for something wonderful happening to me —

A great white hidden tree-root nearby broke the ground to hump like a naked back then opened out to stand up as the risen God (Oh you may be sure He won't arrive in a chariot of fire swooping down among massed crowds of gaping vulgarians!) — this white tree-root remains a disconnected fragment among the memories left over from my coma —

I also remember the vast sky beginning to rock and scatter chaotic light to invade the hearts of the most doubting and shine on their faces dissolving the shadows till the air around us shimmered with flocks of angels' wings while Mr Moloch praised the ancient tree for its fertility and two horses outside the window also broke into light and bats rose as a white glitter of squeaks — leading the prophet to explain sound itself as no more than slow light — oh how the pulsing wings fluttered around and how radiantly the shadows trembled with bass notes and how the whole sky breathed a colossal harmony of C major too massive to be heard! —

Immediately the tree-root and the dazzling harmony of light became part of the soul's holy fervour and I felt myself "an Israelite indeed" and linked my convalescent dreams to my conviction that the Second Coming would happen in the quietest wildest least touched place and He would arrive among us almost unnoticed except for a soft breaking of soil and a sigh of moist mosses — and the more often I dreamed about it the more I found I was the one to say yes that we were ready for the Messiah — so He came to step forward for us to clothe Him in a clean embroidered shirt while Mr Moloch bowed down to the ground in that fawning way of his and took His feet fitting them one at a time with handmade shoes of the finest kid —

The strange part is that in my weakness I dreamed I recoiled a little as if we could smell something faintly evil in the Messiah's paleness — there was a certain hesitancy about His smile of a man wondering whether or not we would forgive *Him* and this seemed curious — there was even an air of evil about the sinuous way He moved — so I suppose I ought to have been warned! —

Neither the leaves in wind nor the ocean away down there nor our creek rushing through the gully when the rains have passed could overwhelm the harmony of light and the tree-root at its centre — nor could those wild parrots swarming among the trees interrupt it — nor the harsh cackle of laughing jackasses — and this was when I understood what my husband meant by Earth storing its light as music — yes he often said Earth stored its light as music — do you like that? —

Mr Moloch — though packed and ready to depart for Melbourne — hung round anxiously and even came to preach at my bedside — he took as his text "Thy light shall rise in obscurity" Isaiah fifty-eight "and thy darkness shall be as the noonday" — I suddenly felt desperate to penetrate what this meant.

Do you know what a consumptive suffers? well the first symptom is a cough — and of course your friends have it too — all at different stages — so everybody is coughing and wherever you go these little coughs and big coughs may be heard — at the dinner table or across the garden or in the dormitory — apologetic but irrepressible coughs — while word flies round that evil thoughts are in the air until this lady or that finds hers taking a turn for the worse.

Well one's chest knots tight in a spasm resisting some enemy pressing a gentle hand there perfectly on the beat — the hand releases you a little when you breathe out only to press more firmly at the next breath — and firmer still at the one after — until it pins you down and you struggle to get out from underneath and fight against suffocation —

Horrible pains fling you about till you are too weak to fight anymore —

Later you bring up ghastly quantities of phlegm (excuse my mentioning this) and you measure the disease as a load which bears ever more heavily on your spirit till you are not fit for work and you disrupt the midnight confessional with uncontrolled coughing so that you suffer the disgrace of your failing twice over — especially because surely a *man* would not be ill with so disgusting an over-abundance of illness —

Then one morning you wake in a drenching sweat — you have shrunk to the size of a stone — helpless against the desperate seizures of coughing — the hand which had remained pressing on your chest for months is now thrust down your throat — stuck — until in a paroxysm you finally retch it up and discover blood on your handkerchief —

It is difficult not to give way to feeling depressed — so very few sufferers do manage to come through and they seem to be those who catch it young —

Although the entire household has noticed you losing weight does a single person venture on the truth to point this out? their manners are too refined if you please! they feel they are left with little they can do but pray — how fervently a sufferer herself prays also in the panic and the secrecy of thoughts too lethal to be put into words —

Without a government medical officer in the area — this was well before Dr von Lossberg's time — what kind of help could be called post haste from Bunda or anywhere inside a hundred miles of Bunda? with the port at Cuttajo not yet built and all the services you take for granted including the telegraph still to come? — it is true that Martha Sparrow had been a nurse and midwife but how could she help when it came to treating scarred lungs and chronic inflammation?

So there you are in bed being watched over by poor

Lavinia — a perpetual fleck of dribble at the corner of her mouth which she wipes away when she thinks to — using one fastidious finger —

And there you remain too lethargic to rouse yourself though somebody keeps coming in to insist that you are needed outside to help dig a well because the work is so slow and that your selfishness will be punished — while day drifts into night and you perspire more than ever until by morning you have to strip off your damp sheets for washing and hang them out to dry or there will be the humiliation of being made to confess your problem plus the anguish of watching one or another of your friends singled out and punished for causing your misfortune — because as I have said already if something goes wrong somebody must have made it go wrong — there always has to be an inner cause for every outward manifestation — or what would be the point of our faith? —

At last voices begin to talk behind your back saying you look as light as a skeleton — you long to contradict them and explain the truth that you feel heavy beyond human endurance but this would be too provoking even if it were physically possible — and in any case you are falling into such a feverish doze you cease to register the difference between night and day while fearful headaches clamp your head and blood thunders and lightnings flash along your nerves and a wind blows through your bones although you doze by chance for a few minutes during which Tuesday merges into Thursday week —

This is what I underwent with the consumption and I am sure it was the same for others — I have heard it said that illness makes a person interesting — though I cannot imagine how! —

Not until Mr Moloch finally decided I would survive and so he could decently leave on his trip to Melbourne did the hateful thing which had invaded my body and threatened my soul for months gradually begin to withdraw — worried faces broke into tired smiles around me as he wished me goodbye and assured me he would return soon from the Ballarat with a title deed to our new mission property in his hand —

I felt giddy and ached in every bone —

Then he was gone and I could smell a disgusting staleness on my skin — I wondered if he had smelt it too as he bent to kiss my brow — oh I wanted him back so I could present myself sweet with soap — but I heard the outer door bang and his footsteps crunching away down the rough road while in the distance a bell was being rung on deck to announce the imminent departure of the packet — and I slumped back on my pillows with the gruesome conviction that I would die after all —

What sprang to mind was a vivid memory of the first time I walked out with him in Stroud — taken aback by his sudden familiarity now we were betrothed — not to mention a manner so assured as to be almost tyrannical — we made our way at his direction — to the tannery —

My poor nose! a nauseous stench poisoned the air

for a distance and the closer we approached the more ghastly — so intense it squeezed the stomach — but what troubled me more was a little matter I could never have mentioned in those polite days — one's mouth fills with saliva even while the living flesh shudders at contact with the ultimate enemy — the charnel house — I was fainting with nausea and leant so heavily on the preacher's arm (whom anyone from our circle would have immediately mistaken as my seducer) that he had to carry me under the grim brick arch and in among stained walls — you know the kind of place? — verdigrised taps dripping — pools of brown blood swimming with bristles — and strange gobbets of viscous membranes touched with a blue sheen and showing veins —

I held my skirts as clear as seemliness would allow but imagine my ankles turning on the cobbles! and the risk of falling!

The workmen knew my companion and acknowledged him for the most part sullenly while they stared at me and made no attempt to spare my modesty or restrain their amazement that I was intruding on their world —

The stench of what they did made me gasp and gag — delving into the pit of my lungs to press against my entrails and butt up against my heart — I felt invaded — my flesh being soured and polluted — blood contaminated — the stench stuck to my hair and plugged my pores leaving the skin sticky and tear ducts gummed up — my stomach turned and bile rose tainted —

though all this was nothing compared to the shame of seeing the preacher mortified by my weakness —

Looking back our tannery visit seems like a trial being survived by somebody else —

The arrangement of the yard was rather in the fashion of a cloister with thick wooden pillars supporting an upper storey — the ground floor where the men worked under shelter at sloping tables remained open — so all round us were labourers bending and straining at their violent task as they scoured cow skins to scrub away a curd of raw fat and blood — drudging with their sleeves rolled above the elbow to show arms roped with horrible veins and while some looked up at me tipping back their cloth caps to show leering faces flushed an ugly dark red others mutely bent again to work with renewed violence —

Have you ever suffered the sort of period of repeated nightmares when even during the daylight hours you can't contemplate bed without cringeing from the terrors almost certainly awaiting you and yet you feel drawn to sleep by desperate overtiredness? — this was how the tannery affected me as if I knew it already and had already found myself unable to escape the shackles of sleep that held me prisoner there — I could have left him and run away home to safety yet I did not —

As it was we walked in through a second archway with me stumbling on the step because I was so frightened by the gloom — missing my balance and going down on one knee while I clutched at the damp wall — well no amount of surreptitious wiping could rid my hand of the contamination of that contact — but already worse and more urgent horrors confronted us with the shapes of whole flattened-out beasts being plunged in a pit full of bubbling liquid where they puffed up to wallow and loom among others being hoisted out (the skins doubly heavy for the fact that they streamed with putrefaction) to be slapped on cobbles and shown as the scraggy remains they were and then dragged away in a welter of nauseous steamy smells to the scourers we had just left —

Seeing how feeble I was my escort hurried me off into a gas chamber where the workmen who looked after this stage of the process were concealed by hanging sheepskins so only their boots could be seen moving along the rows — "Hung out to rot until the wool loosens and falls away" he explained — and added "valuable wool" giving me an odd look as I recall (perhaps the reason for this was that he could only see my eyes since I muffled the rest of my face in a handkerchief) — even so he saw enough to realize my retching had been brought to a crisis "Not in here!" he whispered furiously and dragged me to a little lane connecting the factory's inner and outer buildings just in time to be ahead of the next spasm — the irresistible spasm — during which he looked the other way.

No — my impression was that he felt impatient to get on with the business though he did have the grace to offer me his arm as we climbed a flight of wooden stairs to reach the heart of the operation and stepped right among the most clotted billows of the stink which so sickened the surrounding districts —

The entrails of those dead domesticated servile and mostly female beasts — their spongy glands and heaving lungs — had been boiled into gas until the residue of it smeared every surface of this male world — every greasy wall and step — every lump of machinery slicked with viscous fattiness thudding away with a sweating secretive intestinal heat — the gas like a collective spirit of the slaughtered slicked every surface — a corruption and at the same time a clinging skin —

Fellows in long aprons dipped poles into a line of vats hauling out slimy hides naked of fur and slithering with greenish creamy ripples that seemed supple enough to be another form of life altogether and — watching the men lean back on their heels their faces puffed with concentration — I was once again struck by the ugliness of male strength — their eyes showed raw pink around cold blue pupils and drops of sweat hung from moustaches — their stubbly chins were tucked against shiny creased necks while the pungency of what they created welled beyond description — one of the ogres leaned on his pole to call mockingly "Tell us is there any hope for us in Heaven John?" — another grinned at me around his broken teeth and uttered the word "oak" nodding at the vat —

"Boiled oak for tanning" the preacher translated —

"Dog" the ogre pointed helpfully across to the other vat where some dwarfs were adding ingredients and then standing to watch a moment with glazed eyes — trails of sweat trickling from their hair to run down across their bulging foreheads —

"For softening the finest leathers" the preacher explained "a warm mixture" then hastily led the way down some stairs flush to the far wall and stepped into a room on the next level where he headed straight for a fat old man pulling chamois skins from a giant drum set on its side and being mechanically turned by a system of chains on cogs — he flapped each skin before consigning it to a stack —

Liquid dripped on his boots but I dared not speculate what this liquid might be while watching him extract a desirable item to drape over a sill and then wipe his hands on buttery flanks by way of preparation for leading us past presses where hundreds of skins were being squeezed under heavy blocks and out along a gallery with daylight streaming among racks of spreadeagled animal shapes — every one as flat as paper —

Our conference was to be held here and I gasped the open air with relief — legs shaking and head pulsing — so rather than offer myself for introduction I hung back to stare at those flat outlines larger than life with their crucified limbs — while buyer and seller passed samples from one to another for assessing between finger and thumb — and for reassessing until the choicest skin at last was found to be fine enough for Judge Honeywood's new shoes —

Only then did the truth hit me (a truth I suppose I have always been too mortified to confess to anybody) that this might be the price my suitor had agreed to pay for me!

I shut my eyes to save seeing actual money change hands though I knew quite well that the money was only part of the curdling in my heart which I believed (wrongly) would never go away — well because there was no answer to why a miracle-worker could not have worked the further miracle of obtaining family consent without a bribe of shoes for the rich man who was to appoint my father to a comfortable living — the whole squalid transaction suddenly clear — I believed absolutely in my preacher's gift of levitation and I believed absolutely that he could perform whatever other marvel might suit him — so there must be something I did not understand —

The tannery was worse than the worst ordeal I could have imagined — and I still had to survive the journey out again to the street —

Feeling giddy I leaned against some shelves scarcely bothering to check how filthy they might be — I felt soiled beyond rescue — breathing the slippery stench with its iridescent sheen — the novelty was that my suitor sounded gay and tender when he came to warn me we must return the way we came — I felt his hand on my waist for the first time — though I was afraid of him I knew then that he was to be mine —

"You brought a real little lady there" the dealer remarked to give us the satisfaction of hearing lascivious envy in his voice —

Away we went among muggy fumes down rows of split sheepskins and flattened-wide lizards dangling by a wire through their eye-sockets while behind us the fat man slammed his iron drum shut with a terrific clangour by way of comment (so I thought) and set the shaft turning — steam hissing round his feet — until the whole contraption rumbled and chugged — from the opposite direction a wheelbarrow came bowling towards us pushed by a pale boy of no more than ten — I wondered what had become of Lord Shaftesbury's new law but dared not open my mouth —

I noticed the barrow full of dung —

"From dogs" my friend confirmed with a pleasant nod as he raised the rolled hide he had purchased and sniffed it exactly the way he had put his nose to the inner side of my wrist at our last meeting — then became brisk and faced me about for the ordeal of wending our way again through that maze of horrors   "The vanity of the flesh" he explained while supporting my elbow with an insistent hand "is skin deep — thus I have shown you the skin and all that its beauty amounts to — so now I shall lead you through life — out into fresh air — which is as much as to say that the Lord has chosen me to set your spirit free."

Day after day in my convalescent bed at Yandilli I dreamed the same odious memory until at last I slept without dreaming and woke to a cavernous appetite —

I am told the colour had swept back into my cheeks and that day by day I could be seen to gain strength — the worst was behind me and Mr Moloch would be gone for at least another month — birds sang! ladies chattered and coughed quietly! my nightmare of errors evaporated in the sunny air — I came to my senses blissfully afloat in clear morning light while the discarded darkness sank down like an insect's horny casing folded away —

I had returned to life exhausted and I knew that — though I would survive my illness — something far more deeply troubling was afoot — was in fact happening in my body — something growing assertive as the consumption weakened —

Signs were soon manifest —

Unmistakably I was expecting a child — I knew nothing about it! I was terrified disgusted guilty baffled and disbelieving! what's more I would soon find myself faced with an impossible task — how could such news be broken to my husband on his return (no matter how passionately I might declare my innocence) without branding me a wanton?

No one can despise my cowardice more than I —

Let me assure you it is still mortifying to look back on after all these years — especially considering the way I taunted myself to the point of contemplating a fatal accident (my own) only to be discovered dozing with a smile on my face — and woken out of a dream in which Mr

Moloch was the one who met with the fatal accident —
on his sea voyage home from the goldfields —

Remember Beatrice Offley's interpretations? — a day
was indeed a thousand years — and if fear is not necessarily love — beyond question love can be fear!

The saintly Lavinia kept bursting into my room like a
lunatic — by turns interrogating me about my lapses of
faith "Why are you swallowing your pill — the space you
leave — what is that dratted word — trumpets — swallowing your medicine — I mean — surrendering —
yes!" only to collapse on her knees to sob on my breast —
where she would be found by Hester (the evil Hester)
arriving in from doing the garden to offer me solicitude
and to provide herself with another opportunity for eyeing
me closely —

I had to keep my secret from everyone — not even Ann
could be told something so unnatural — anyhow it might
prove to be hysteria — maybe the radiance I felt would
simply go away — and I prayed that it might.

Can you imagine what it is like to be a lady dreaming of having a stronger body than a man? this was how powerfully the tide of recovery flowed through me — so that I fell to wondering about the others and whether they also entertained shameful fantasies while serving tea and primly dabbing their lips with table napkins —

We were all from good families — you see — and this would have made us oddities in Melbourne let alone Yandilli where our library was enough to arouse deep suspicion not to mention the grand pianoforte — talk about oddities! — nothing like us had been seen before in this raw heat of a forgotten little port on the east coast of Nowhere —

I was soon out and about and able to participate in the gentler pursuits — my easel set up among the rest and my paintbrush jiggling in the water jar while I frowned at an inadequate sketch of *Platycircus elegans* the matchless rosella (it is so important to give everything its proper name don't you agree?) and this was fun enough for a while — pleasant despite Ann's habit of spilling her jar and despite our nagging worries concerning Flora — Flora had come down with my disease but seemed to be enjoying no such revival — while we painted the crimson plumage of that shot bird propped up before us (shot by my husband as a parting gift) our thoughts wandered back to a shallow grave in the stones of Ascension Island — the screams of a million angry seabirds wheeling about us like a cyclone —

With our poor pinch of skill we struggled hopelessly with landscapes copied from Constable — just as we laboured in Schubert's wake at the pianoforte — and don't mention our attempts at emulating the divine Jane with embryonic novels set among our memories of Stroud! though I suppose the harmless twinge of failure is what one means by "having a jolly time" —

The jolly time was darkened by taking turns to sit at Flora's bedside — and by several others beginning to cough seriously — then came a period of weeks when we were confined indoors during bad weather with the coughs becoming more strident — we sewed and cooked while accepting that the gales would delay Mr Moloch for at least another week — furious squalls sent low clouds trailing torn edges among the bent trees — rain lashed the mission completely flattening our garden and yet (such

paradoxical creatures women are) we felt ridiculously
lighthearted at being left a little longer to our own devices —

Tenderness grew among us — beginning perhaps with
caring for Flora — whatever the cause we softened and
talked among ourselves about other things than salvation
and duty until we reached the stage where all but me
took to embracing (I dared not in my secret condition)
and the sharp words of our vocabulary fell out of use —

Even making allowances for my unique problem I realize I did behave rather more pettishly than necessary
and set myself rather too publicly apart — making it hard
for them to forgive me later — the idea did not once
enter my head that we might someday learn from this
month of tenderness or look back on our period without
a man at the mission for hints as to the way life might
change permanently for the better.

I sat apart while the other ladies showed off their education — embroidering slaves and factory children —
tuning our pianoforte because the instrument was in great
demand not only for hymn singing but when they treated
the wallabies to some Haydn trios or Edwina and Hester
scared the rosellas off our crops with Chabrier's transcrip-
tion of the "Eroica" — they sang Thomas Weelkes mad-
rigals with the bass line picked out on a cello and the
tenor sung by Elizabeth Eyre who could manage anything
down to E — then Elizabeth was joined by Charlotte
declaiming bits of Shakespeare's histories at Flora's bed-

side — and the sick Flora herself with her feeble voice pluckily dismissed Zeno's paradox of Achilles and the tortoise — mainly she said from moral repugnance on behalf of that bewildered reptile fleeing ahead of the beastly Achilles for interminable ages by ever diminishing degrees —

It all comes back to me now — the sheer miracle of not having to cut short these dizzy pleasures in routine self-surrender at confessionals which had been known to last well into the night — peeling away the layers under Mr Moloch's leadership — excuse this cough — each laying bare some crime of petty shortcomings — excuse me — exposing a flayed soul as pathetic as our bruised ugly bodies — before we could settle down together round the kitchen table for a nice hot cup of chocolate and a chat about tomorrow's tasks in the vegetable garden — well it would be soon enough to resume confessionals when the prophet returned —

A letter arrived to say he would be on his way directly and giving a date but that very day Flora complained of frightful pains in her marrow — the horror of her crisis was what broke me from keeping aloof and finally drove me off my convalescent couch — unable to lie helplessly in hearing of her gasps because no medicines were any help at this stage and nothing but death would staunch her flow of murmurings — I had to be up so I could creep away into my own peace —

I took to waiting in the front room — standing at the

window gazing out to sea (with the pretence of watching for the flag to be hoisted at the jetty to announce the packet's arrival) because for me the sea represented freedom — in wild weather or fine — and to be honest it also represented home — contact with sweet moments of the life I led as a girl in a Gloucestershire town watching the maid scatter damp tea leaves on our floor and then sweep up the dust in little balls —

Nothing can be done for consumption except rest and Flora did rest — but I was growing too robust to quell my agitation — part of it being the strength given me by that inexplicable pregnancy and the baby just big enough to be felt with my cold hands — I stood at the window and willed my husband not to come home — never to come home.

Don't you remember the shipwreck? don't you remember the cyclone and those frightful gales when roofs blew off? then you must have been down with chickenpox or something of the kind — you never saw such a drama once the packet went missing and everybody guessed she must be in trouble —

My perverse heart went out to Mr Moloch — seasick as he must be — who had gone away on his errand purely to satisfy my demand —

I felt most terribly powerful and at the same time most terribly ashamed to think that on my say-so he would probably also imagine he could calm the storm — and with more days of suffering ahead if the captain decided to stand offshore until the weather improved —

Some other ladies came in to join me at the window until it quite fogged up with our breath —

We muffled ourselves in outdoor clothes though this was still early morning and the new wild day had not long drifted ashore as an eerie mist — light positively billowed in to push away the dark and blind the town with luminous whiteness — broken by glimpses now and again of foam thick with flotsam being dashed to fragments surging among the jagged rocks —

Even though I had felt more lonely with my husband by my side than with him away I said to myself — disgustedly at that time — "You are infested with love!"

Imagine our shock when some person banged on the back door — who ever came near us? — we were considered out of bounds — he shouted his news that the packet had missed the mouth of the bay altogether! — while I stood paralysed I felt Earth turn because my husband was the only person alive who could question the legitimacy of the child I apparently had to have —

I pulled myself together — though still terribly weak — ordered horses harnessed in the sulkies for collecting whatever farm machinery Mr Moloch might bring home — two completely unknown boys helped us — and within minutes we were driving along to Yandilli wharf — close though it was — the boys riding on our tailboards — long before we'd found places for our horses at the hitching rail we were drenched —

Ghosts of the future were already with me — strapping a gag over my mouth and nose — already sticking pins into my palms and already squeezing my heart —

The crowd of jostlers knew the worst of course — some going off to saddle their horses and others begging rides in carts — while hampered by clumsy rain capes we struggled back into our own sulkies and drove to the crossroads — by this time I had forgotten we didn't belong — being among so many worried folk — and you would never have thought more than a dozen families lived in the district! — all as swaddled up in their outer garments as we were in our guilts — nothing showing but tense white faces with pinched mouths — eyes wide enough to see right in from helplessness to helplessness —

The pandemonium itself was sufficient to put a person in a panic — boots thudding and wheels squealing — not to mention some child letting out hair-raising howls against the gale — when it came to the point just the wind alone could deafen you like a higher pitch of silence — yet in the middle of all this I found a moment for telling myself "I am an unhappy person" — miserable little drab — as if I mattered! — while horses panted and iron-bound wheels grated on and on among popping stones along a road recently cut through some scrub — trees swirled for all the world like desperate things trying to ward off the sky — and loosed dozens of mad black hunchbacked cockatoos to sweep across our path letting out witches' shrieks —

Cuttajo cliffs are as sombre and uncouth a place as

mortal might ever wish to find — we waited there among
neighbours we had never said much more to than a hasty
"Good morning" — your own folk among them I have
no doubt — O'Donovans and McNeils — as well as those
Earnshaw men looking more handsome than expected —
talking to a fellow whose name I never knew though I
would recognize his face anywhere because his casual conversation struck me at the time as a very great kindness —
also the giant son of the Irish convict next door — oh
and who else?

Poor exclusive outcasts that we were — we savoured
this tragic hour of shivering among familiar strangers as
the rain pelted down — catching sight of Mr Moloch's
ship in time to watch her sink behind breakers with only
her bare masts in view — shreds of canvas flapping from
the yards — she canted into the mist as she rose through
a dump of surf — a black wet sidelong senseless shape
just beyond the reef — looming like an object from my
troubled fancy and quite the sort of unsavable something
I lived with all the time — and came on just as if the
rocks were no more than another ridge of the swell —
we saw her bow tip in the air — foam massed and cas-
caded across the deck to sweep over a cluster of humans
swarming down the hull into madly bucking boats —
boats being lifted level with the rail and then a moment
later sucked down lower than the reef where the ship's
keel lodged — then up they'd swoop again — oars at odd
angles and tillers useless — more bodies dropped into

them — though most hesitated a fatal moment and fell
floundering into the surf of breakers instead —

The retribution which hung over me was moving closer
and I knew —

You cannot imagine what horrible jubilation took hold
of me despite myself and my upbringing in the church —

I strove to ward off the blame but more and more I
began to believe I had been dreaming this disaster for
days — and having dreamed it I must have brought it
about — beyond question I had wanted to prevent Mr
Moloch coming home — so great was the pressure of this
guilt that I confided in Ann (though I made no mention
of my baby) — whispering into her dripping ear there
and then on the cliffs — while whips of escaped hair cut
at our faces — only to be scolded for my sin of pride —

Among all the ladies at the mission Ann was probably
alone in having no axe to grind — she said the whole
catastrophe was too big to be my fault —

We shrieked till our voices grew ragged — calling in
vain "Mr Moloch Mr Moloch!" — before following Charlotte Smith's lead (more about dear Lotte the conniver
later) singing "Eternal Father strong to save" — we sang
it out — "O hear us when we cry to Thee For those in
peril on the sea" — and lo and behold against all prob-
ability this worked — because minutes after the last lifeboat went down to be lost the tide rolled a man's body
on to the beach — just one poor puny indestructible
man — we watched him stagger to his feet in the shal-

lows — and all my old helplessness recognized in him
what I did not choose to recognize — that far from wanting to be free of him I wanted him to be exclusively mine
as I was his — and drew me instantly into his orbit —

Can you picture me in my green dress with purple satin
panels and pagoda sleeves which I had foolishly worn with
a view to enchanting Mr Moloch afresh in the event of
the Almighty's failure to strike him dead? when instead
of a husband I was confronted by this miserable creature
who came hobbling through ankle-deep water only to be
buffeted by the next wave swarming up to his waist and
then just as violently swarming back down to drag a mat
of sliding shingles from underfoot — yet it *was* my husband who had survived despite my wickedness you see!
leaving me engulfed under tides of hopelessness — then
a second sodden object rolled in on its tummy and rolled
on its back and rolled on its tummy and finally in despair
was let flop to one side — but the power that sucked all
strength from me suddenly pumped me full of double
energy when the first survivor began wading to the rescue — he blocked the body to stop it sliding out again —
well I dared not think why — so I acted instead —
despite my delicate condition — and promptly led the
way slithering down through wattles and spiny grass
though I felt that knives were gashing me with every
breath I took — oh yes if I ever hoped I had not given
in to love I knew better at that moment — but by the
time I reached him — the seething tide flooding into my

shoes — some Earnshaw men were already respectfully keeping their distance while Mr Moloch in his water-logged suit warded them off from a drowned woman — insisting she was his and his alone to drag ashore.

During my years with the Household of Hidden Stars many's the time I swore to run away and never come back but sure as eggs the moment I took the decision things changed — I would see a brighter side and feel surrounded by affection — besides the faith we had in common — so I would stay — I stayed because I believed in Mr Moloch's special powers too — also thanks to the simple fact that he was a man — if you see what I mean — and the fascination of this — a strange creature with rituals of shaving and fixing his collar stud and a prickly temper — not to mention his vanity in needing to be right especially when he knew he was wrong and especially needing to prove his strength when a task was plainly beyond him — a typical man I think we could say —

As for the vicious things (there were vicious things) I tended to accept them as somehow — well — comfortable because these were only household cruelties — you don't so much mind your arm being pinched or your hair pulled or having to endure cutting remarks when you are trapped together by a country so alien it reeks of fertility and suffocating age — apart from which Ann was always available to cut things down to size with some such comments as "Won't it be more serious if we have a heatwave too?" or "Tell me about it when you've fallen into a ravine and can't climb out!" — then if any of us continued to make a fuss she'd point out that we would have been worse off drowned — or frozen to death — or stuck in a cannibal's stew pot!

Indeed yes some people *were* eaten I have no doubt just as others drowned — we heard tell of a sunken ship just off the reef at Yandilli where the lads used to go diving to prove what men they were and risked their lives to bring back a porcelain dish or two for trophies or a few scraps of lead ballast worth a shilling at most — and you yourself among them at one stage — next thing these same lads went to prove how good they were in the ranges from which if the wind blew from the right quarter we used to hear remote songs of lost souls flying above the high gullies — though what those expeditions were to prove I'm sure I don't know because you young hopefuls had little to show for your pluck apart from plenty of lacerations — unless we count one breathless boy stumbling in through this gate here to tell us he'd found blood spots on a flat rock somewhere up the mountain! I remember every detail you see! and I believe what I was told —

I must pull myself together.

You are surprised by my memory? well we shall see what you think when you hear the things I have been keeping secret in this head of mine — how we faced the

tragedy and how eventually we learned to laugh again —
there's nothing new about tragedy and anger ending in
laughter — even our present arrangement of living in
separate houses has its interesting side — do you think
I don't know what I am talking about? or that I can hear
the clink of crockery from over there without feeling a
savage pain in my heart and a longing to set out on some
long journey — to stand under a beech tree while a thrush
bursts into song overhead — to be free? — because all
my life I have wanted happiness — and yet really I am
such a perfect colonial I shall never go home —

If you think this is not what you came to hear you
shall soon discover how wrong you are —

Let me take you back to the shipwreck and the exhausted Mr Moloch buzzing like a hornet while we
crowded round him   "Keep away! get out!" he shouted
at me and then looked up to address the air above us (like
this) because now he had an argument with God "All
right all right!" which was when I knelt to check the
woman's heart and breathing and found none of either so
she was dead as a stone — and this I would swear in a
court of law —

When I told him she was dead he accused me of desiring
it — which came like a slap in the face because I was his
wife — and not until much later did I come to see that
I *did* desire it and my intuition had told me the truth
about her — so this may give you some idea how well
he understood me — also how he understood that I was

swooning under the pain of watching him stoop over her
and watching his breath of life being breathed into her —
because I at last knew what it would look like to have it
breathed into me instead —

I do not believe he ever came to suspect me of calling
up the storm itself —

You know yourself how treacherous the coast is here
even in fine weather — with sharp rocks under a glitter-
ing mirror of reflections — well that was me and the fury
in my loving heart too — let alone when surges come
fuming inshore and night breaks your sleep with muffled
thunder — don't ask more —

So having slithered on seaweed dollops stinking of io-
dine (without a murmur of complaint even though I could
scarcely stand at that stage so oppressed was I by the
weight of the sky I had to hold up) I came to look upon
this interesting young woman and saw a mere lump of
flesh bandaged in tight fashions all sopping wet — deliciously caught and knotted — you must imagine colourless lips and blue storm smudges and closed eyes and
a nose pinched white at the nostrils — imagine hair fairer
than wheat but darkened by deep water and strapped
round her chin as if while strangling her someone had
also bound it under her jaw and then up over her head
to keep her from calling for help — she looked perhaps
twenty — a year or two older than I — her solid neck
jutted at one end of her dress while at the other a marbled
ankle appearing every bit as obscene stuck into its boot
from which laces snaked with the receding current while

a few flags of seaweed hooked on a bodice button snaked the same way — she made a dramatic impression — you might say she had such training in striking poses that even when dead and without her guidance her body struck this last pose for itself — I was a child being bullied by each new surprise to ask what was expected of me by the older people among whom I had to make my place —

I mention her training because she turned out to be an opera singer — as you shall hear —

Ann arrived muttering against any interference in others' troubles and sniffed at the sight of our prophet crouching down again to place his swarthy cheek on that dead Jezebel's pallid one —

I have already described how Mr Moloch's big mouth big nose and big dark eyes could suddenly come to life with astonishing effect — well there below the cliffs he grew brilliant in just this way and if anybody in creation could raise the dead it was him with his big ear listening to her transparent ear which looked as though she was showing it by the light of day for the first time in her life — his black eyelashes brushed her eyelids —

Do you want to know more?

He was an elusive character and you had to catch him at the right angle to see what he was like at all — if you know what I mean — rather like a Daguerreotype plate on which the image is sometimes vividly clear but then — at the slightest trembling of the hand it may become a mere ghost of itself or be lost altogether —

I should explain that in his darkness he was a child of

sunlight — this was the mystery of it — while in her
pallor she looked to be a netherworld creature only ever
seen by the glow of footlights — and I might add I did
not need shouting at — already weighed down with the
despair of how she brought out more beauty in him than
I ever had except for a private occasion in a vestry which
seemed too long lost to matter anymore — but the point
was we were not alone this time — so once again he
shamed me in public with his violent lack of discretion —
and I became too much caught up in my own miseries
to realize that no one but Ann was watching us — the
rest were frantic figures in oilskins clambering along a
groin of rocks toward large broken boxes which only minutes earlier had been a ship — and then the Earnshaws
found time to step aside a moment to offer us a blanket
for covering the dead which Mr Moloch accepted out of
a misunderstanding because he spread it flat and lay down
on it himself before wrapping the both of them together — him and the woman —

I was totally disgraced —

All I could think to do was look away toward remote
shouts reaching us from the rocks where the rescue party
of fellows pressed ahead laden under coils of rope and
grappling hooks — silhouettes against a blast of white
spray with their balanced arms outstretched while spin-
drift sank from the sky or great feathered sea shapes
clutched at them — and the rearing sea beyond heaved
up another cavernous broken box with two masts still
stuck out of it —

Her world of the theatre was taking over ours —

The next roller flung down a fresh burden and with it the first lifeboat — a nimble sleek upside-down thing — horrifying because it skimmed like a porpoise until the shore party rushed among churning waters in the shallows to secure it and turn it over and display its emptiness while further in the foam several heads still bobbed and were buried under a suffocating thunder of foam —

Birds were blown by the wind with crooked wings and bony pink feet clenched on nothing and beaks gaping while they screeched at us because (poor feeble sinners that we were) we had been no help to anybody and then they were whisked away among the souls of the dead as I've mentioned — up over the forest like heathen creatures calling to Baal who was as big as a whole mountain and blinked his million eyes among the leaves — can you imagine? — the Earth shook each time the ocean was flung against it so we could feel a living anger underfoot while the tempest howled and hurled down torrents of rain to block out all vestige of the hills of "Paradise."

Excuse me.

Yes for all I know there were screams last Monday and for all I know they were mine but this would not have been the first time — and if you still do not understand you should accept that you know little about the true faith in Jesus Christ.

One has to seek perfection from oneself — you are my witness that I am not at all a colourful person though we

live in colourful times — the fact is that things go wrong
and when things go wrong somebody must be to blame —
the worst punishment let me say is to be given hours of
silence and yet one never hears complaints in the district
about silence —

Where was I up to? — I mustn't lose the thread —
yes the mournful cry of gulls blowing about and the wind
tangling our hair as we strained to see if anybody else
might be rescued from the disaster — "O Christ whose
voice the waters heard and hushed their raging at a word"
we sang while figures fit for dreams of happiness teetered
further and further away out along that jagged finger of
land — "who walkest on the foaming deep and calm amid
the storm didst sleep" — to where masts tilted uselessly
and frantic little canvas hands flapped from the yards —

Our shrill voices sang "O hear us when we cry to Thee
For those in peril on the sea" as we glimpsed other rags
in the pounding waves being churned under — jumbled
about brutally with limbs and trunks still in them or dead
arms flung up or hands lacking bodies — I felt how pathetic we were and how daft a creature God had bred in
us — do you see our waterlogged bonnets with the quill-
ing spoiled? bodies clutched by cold dresses? well this
was what we were reduced to while we apologized for
upsetting Mr Moloch and backed away murmuring self-
effacements which could not possibly have aggravated
even the most sensitive of bullies while he cupped that
stranger's head in his hands and a cry broke from him to
coil away like the crack of a whip —

Then I'm telling you we saw her body flip over of its
own accord convulsing free of his grasp — kicking off
his blanket — and heaving while her smooth statue's face
flushed dark as a plum to vomit a bucket of clear stuff
for each spasm that doubled her up —

Womenfolk from Yandilli township and from "Paradise" came sloshing and flummoxing our way (I cannot
put it better than that and you will know what I mean
with your mother one among them) gathering their skirts
and managing baskets of food for nothing better than
rescuing Muley Moloch's opera singer who might have
been his paramour too for all we knew — small wonder
I felt ashamed of my husband's ignorance concerning the
decorum expected of a churchman — yes she was a common opera singer —

Martha handed him a flask of brandy — Hester offered
to take the drowned female's arm and help her up —
Charlotte of course offered the same service on the other
side — I accused him bitterly saying "All the time you
were away I had you and only you on my mind" (yet I
dared not admit my guilty reason) —

In that uncivilized place my aloneness was brought
home to me by his cold stare and tightening mouth —
I knew I must face ostracism — even among those close
enough to me not to feel outright horror at the sight of
my pregnancy —

Yet I was not inclined to submit without a fight — I
neither liked the bond between him and this new individual nor felt called upon to disguise my dislike — I

threw it at him that I would be grateful to move away from the port into obscurity — pointing inland as I did so — and then I looked up in that direction to emphasize my anger — only to see a strange figure perched on the cliff — head like a little black tent supported by three flimsy stick legs and two sturdy human legs —

A single round expressionless eye observed us —

I said to myself "This is the end of the world we know — nothing can be private ever again!" and I recall thinking "Yet there will be no more lies because every fact can be proved from now on" — no more crime — out loud I said "Let's for goodness' sake hurry!" — hearing Hester ask was the thousand-year kingdom to be entirely photographed? while she and Charlotte laboured under the weight of assisting that huge pale Goth of his — "May I introduce" he remembered his manners ridiculously "Miss Louisa Theuerkauf?" —

I had already turned my back — it was no concern of mine that she looked half dead and not fit to travel for a long time — I could find no room for mercy — we had planned on going straight into the hills to claim our new property so that is what we would do — promptly next morning — I told myself I did not care if the journey killed her.

What a wind! what clouds! anyone would think the sky is flapping away to China it's in such a hurry.

Yes there are simple answers to your questions because

every question does have a simple — but this won't help you understand what you are asking — not a bit — I cannot possibly give you answers just like that until I have taken you right back to the beginning so you'll at least have some idea what they mean —

As for religion *this* is my religion — these shacks and hovels that hold the relics of our hopes — bless you — certainly I shall show you around in a few minutes although you'll remember the mission I dare say —

Not much changes apart from bits falling off and roofs leaking — yes that building was the prayer hall when you were here and except for the couple of pews we chopped up for firewood during the recent floods it remains pretty much the same —

The worst things I suffer are in my mind — much worse than the shortage of breath — chronic though that is — left over from the white plague —

Those were the stables down there though all except one of the horses died of melancholy — but you know enough about our stables — doesn't it make you hoot to think how cluttered we are with things decaying before they even have time to get old? (including me!) well we are a puzzle to ourselves for sure and in my opinion this is thanks to the fact that the moment people think of something sensible they do the opposite! what else!

Proof? what more proof do you need than *us* trailing out here although we had been settled comfortably in our cottages at Yandilli? — maybe we need never have

moved — because the point is that when I went slithering
down that muddy slope to the beach — acutely aware
that nobody knew how petrified I was of jolting the baby
in my womb — I vowed to put all our plans at risk —
though I didn't care if the journey inland killed Louisa
Theuerkauf I cared that my baby might be born in guilt
if his secret remained a secret — so clearly I should take
the punishment on myself and tackle the problem straight
away —

For a while I weakened — something had happened to
me beyond my control that disgraced me and soiled me
(despite the fact that it also filled my blood with fire) —
maybe the true alternative was not a confession but an
earnest prayer for the Almighty to strike us all dead in
His vengeance! —

Yet when I lost my balance momentarily my whole life
sprang alert with the need to protect the baby — wasn't
the baby's safety the very reason I had been more shocked
by seeing my husband stand in the foam than by seeing
him washed around like a corpse? — I returned to the
nausea of my decision to let the truth out so it could
never be taken back — to be free of it — so as I say I
was rushing over the brittle shells towards my husband
and heedless of his own extremity I opened my mouth to
cry out "I am with child!" —

He cut me short before I could utter a sound — he
looked up from the drowned creature at his feet and
shouted right in my face "Keep away! get out!"

*   *   *

Imagine a string of five vehicles — four sulkies and a spring cart — ready to set off from Yandilli to carry us inland to this place which we had purchased with Edwina's money but which none of us had seen — our guide being the young Irish giant from next door who drove the leading vehicle in which Flora's mattress had been put and Flora lifted up to lie on it — then Mr Moloch helped his invalid opera singer on to the step and climbed in beside her — leaving me to manage as best I may —

The owner clipped the tailboard in place with the special care of a man made proud by his brand-new equipment and then stepped up with us and took the reins —

My husband sat defiantly while the meaning of that defiance pierced me to the heart — and I took my place facing them — determined never to take my eyes off them — to save my dignity and because of the contempt I felt for them — determined not to let my suffering show —

Flora gave out a few murmurs and when neither of the others appeared interested in listening I leaned down (still watching them) to ask what she wanted — "Did Beatrice die" she pleaded in gasps "because she argued with the prophet?" — it frightened me — yet I knew without meeting her eyes that she meant my husband to answer —

"Flora asks" I shot her words at him with so much venom I astonished myself "did Beatrice die because she defied you?" and the sulky jolted into motion while the driver's back listened to us — we went bumping down over a gutter and swung up along the smooth road — the Goth wobbled imperturbably — Mr Moloch's silence concentrated in his eyes as an exceptional power while he stared me down with that brilliant dark look of his — to Flora he said nothing — even when she put out a feeble hand and held on to his shoe —

All along the high street folk watched us pass — you could hear how glad they were to see us go by the greetings they called to Mr Jack Earnshaw who drove the second sulky (the other one with passengers — Ann Lavinia Charlotte and the two Elizabeths) — the three buggies loaded with our furniture and tools were in the hands of Hester and Martha and Lady Edwina —

The rude priest who used to be at Yandilli in those days stood at the door of his iron church and drew the only words we heard from our driver "Morning Father" the giant called and then mumblingly reproved us for our lack of respect "Father O'Shaughnessy don't you know?" — young Billy McNeil was struggling with the blinds to help open up his parents' butchery — and I fancy we may even have seen you holding your mother's hand because we certainly saw her — she crossed herself — her superstition made me want to stop the pony and leap out and shake her! — in that same moment my mind filled with mutiny at the likelihood that Beatrice had died thanks to the resentment I felt whenever she put

my husband in his place as a man who could neither read
nor write —

Then we were out in the country and quite suddenly
overhung by trees from which trailing vines brushed our
shoulders and twigs snagged our woollen jackets — the
road shrank to a track jostling us roughly and the sound
of hooves was muffled by soft evil silt while our wheels
lurched against roots and skidded into potholes — I felt
awfully queasy and headachy — the air filled with such
huge shadows we ducked and shielded our heads against
them — all except the opera singer who had made a remarkable recovery overnight —

Louisa Theuerkauf was firmly determined I should feel
her resentment at my watching her — which meant she
must have recognized my *right* even in the absence of
anyone pointing me out or explaining my special status
as the wife — though indeed she worked herself round
to half face my husband so he could not help seeing how
she registered neither surprise nor apprehension at finding
herself driven into a wilderness (a reminder that she had
been to her death in order to follow him so what else was
there to fear?) but she also faced him so he could not help
watching her cut me out from the silent communications
they shared under cover of indifference nor fail to catch
the quirky tilt of her chin when some thought came into
her head which she intended imparting by telepathy —
not to mention what meaning there might have been in
that intense possessive questioning frigid look of hers —

We trundled out of the tunnel of leaves into sparser bush with splashes of sunshine on the ground — an eerie sense of expectation filled the air — and I realized that if once you were to be lured into leaving the track you would never find it again — all the trunks being identical and identically spaced — no horizon visible or anything beyond the trees themselves — you would be lost in five minutes —

Never was there any place so shapeless or nameless or bewilderingly closed against being understood — even the birds swooped around in silence — "Mr Moloch has said" Flora hissed at me from the floor as several bumps threw her about among shafts of pain "we must beware the Devil and all his works!" even her weak voice sounded too loud in this brooding place —

I hoped our land at the mission would be different —

The prophet neglected Flora perhaps because he felt helpless to cure her — I don't know — however at last the Goth condescended to stare down at her coldly — showing about as much tact as a mincing machine — meanwhile they both continued to ignore me and left it to me to console the poor creature besides looking after my own fragile health —

By contrast Mr Moloch frequently enquired after the Goth's comfort and her restored strength or such trivialities as her satisfactory placement in regard to the wind if you please! the amazing thing was that her vulgar coquettishness appeared to escape him even while she

made use of sunlight and shadow much as if they were
stage lighting which she turned to such marvellous effect
that her unmoving face appeared animated by constant
variety so flickers of brilliance darted in the corner of a
still eye and her large simple cheek was endlessly re-
moulded by the changeable glow and veiling —

The previous day's storm having dispersed left the air
entirely cleansed so as to seem too neutral to sustain life —
broken grass lay combed out along the verges — our
guide drove undaunted along a track never better than
greasy and sometimes completely under puddles — the
pony appeared in positively carnival mood skittishly kicking up its heels and flattening its ears —

Voices carried from the other sulkies — little clusters
of conversation budding on the passing air and briefly
flowering — but in ours any such effort withered under
the tensions created by our driver's disapproval (eloquently
expressed by the most massive back I had ever seen) and
the angers passing mutely from one side of the sulky to
the other — not to mention Flora between — letting out
desperate groans which she had abandoned all attempt to
suppress —

By lunchtime we reached the tall trees and I decided
maybe we *were* lost — the track becoming drier and ston-
ier the wheels rhythmically jounced us about with such
relentless violence I longed to cry out "For goodness' sake
stop right here and let us at least get down and walk!"
but shame kept me from complaining and I could not tell

whether the others (who were not in my condition) might have been enjoying it — meanwhile the lofty gloom struck me as not just hostile but hostile in a queerly challenging way — so untouched by civilization and having a certain grandeur of senselessness (yet if you had told me I might someday surrender to it like one intoxicated I would have laughed in your face) — leafage loosened during the storm pattered around us and settled as a cushion to muffle the dainty hooves padding along —

In the sheer wildness of that era we must have been an astonishing advent — our procession of bonnets and fluttering mantles — our fragments of laughter —

Although we felt a great deal of apprehension about the future we also felt relief at leaving Yandilli brooding on its past of scorched walls and ruined outbuildings — besides I need hardly tell *you* that two years in a tiny seaside village in New South Wales is quite enough to addle the brain and altogether squash the gaiety from one's animal spirits — you have been here a whole lifetime after all —

So we were escaping — yes — but at the same time we knew this put us beyond reach of help — including the doctor's help (though I dared not commiserate with Flora on such a matter because I dared not explain myself) — we had trotted far out of sight of the last pasture and up among boulders — joggling and shuddering over ruts to wend our way through a forest rising

on all sides and cloaking the ranges like the gigantic
rustling waves of an unbroken sea —

Down into a gully we swayed with overtaxed springs
thumping against the frame and into a stream — watching the following carts crawl and slew as they set my
friends rocking and holding on — also hearing Jack Earnshaw sing out to us that this was called Burnt Bridge
Creek — well we could have done with a bridge because
we stuck halfway across! — our driver cooed at the pony
and clicked his tongue to encourage it and murmured
endearments which came strangely from so taciturn a
specimen while the poor beast heaved and trembled without success — eventually the fellow jumped down to put
his own shoulder to the wheel — give him his due —
immediately we lurched out of the hole we were in and
bounced up the slope with him striding beside — boots
spouting water and trousers sopping — he only jumped
back on when we reached the crest —

In this country sons are always taller than their fa-
thers — but I might say he was providentially ugly —

On the hill climb to the summit I wondered about that
burnt bridge and when it might have been burnt —
surely precious few civilized folk had settled this district
before us? the question let a draught into my soul —

We trundled along the top making better progress
despite many diagonal gutters across the track which
caused us such discomfort I believe Flora several times
lost her senses —

Louisa merely adjusted the set of her head to present her brow for the green shade to accentuate her majestic mound of hair which she wore swept up in the secular style — the changes deepened her eyes —

Please do not think I intend sounding spiteful — nor that I am taking a belated opportunity to pitch into her — I simply have to tell what I remember as I remember it — everything matters —

When we came upon a solitary hut in a clearing I feared it might be our new home but as we drew closer we could read a sign over the door *The Brian Boru Inn* — the publican came out to salute our guide — evidently expecting anyone who passed that way to stop — however Mr Moloch insisted we keep moving and refused to sanction even five minutes' rest for the ponies at so sinful a place (this was before the establishment moved to the new village of Cuttajo) — so we pressed on — hearing Jack Earnshaw's voice call a greeting and the publican's answer like a lonely echo — up the winding stony track in a gulch with a perilous drop inches from our wheel — we were heading north now and when the trees thinned we were surprised to find we could still catch glimpses of the sea —

Nobody can tell what will lead to what — you may trace any catastrophe back to issues of dwindling importance until you reach some miserable bubbling spring so feeble you could plug it by sticking your hand in — and the same with each tributary of the river — well here is an issue of little importance to start from —

As soon as our leader agreed to a break the ponies gathered to wheeze together with the sulkies standing at odd angles — Martha drove up in the last one complaining that her vehicle had no springs while ours was new — and read aloud the freshly painted lettering on our tailboard "Paradise" — "Oh Mr Moloch" she tittered "you are there already!" —

I have no reason to suppose she was commenting on the fact that my husband sat beside Louisa Theuerkauf — nor that Martha intended any unkind comment on my being obliged to face them and watch them sway together (despite the good springs) shaken by the same jolts — but if somebody had told me then that Louisa and I would one day live together and that she would lead me to freedom — well! —

"Look!" called Ann from the next sulky "is that a grave?" and she pointed among the moss-grown tree trunks — unmistakably there was a mound of newly heaped soil and leaves —

"Grave?" Flora croaked in alarm from where she lay too weak even to prop herself up on one elbow "Why would anyone be buried out here?" and added "unless they were murdered?" —

The prophet stared dumbly at the mound but Farmer Earnshaw smiled and explained that it was the nest made by a forest bird — a kind of turkey — and that the mound of mulch was for keeping the eggs warm — Muley Moloch decided against a sermon on that occasion so he sat down abruptly and ordered the Irishman to drive on.

* * *

In the mid-afternoon we arrived — or at least we came
to a gate where we stopped — I believe we all felt a little
like trespassers even though we knew the Barnetts had
already moved out —

But not Louisa —

Stillness watched us — stillness listened to us — and
Stroud seemed far enough away for Miss Honeywood to
have been no more than a witch in a fairy tale — yet at
that instant I was overpowered by nostalgia for the lawn
at the Hall where I used to sit among daisies on the clipped
grass — nothing seemed more unlikely than that we ourselves might have just such a lawn here one day —

Of course our new mowing machine was in among the
luggage but Mr Moloch felt so tremendously proud of it
he had not been able to bring himself to soil it with work
in two years — maybe because his ideal lawn had to be
somewhere permanent — as a promise of gentility —

We gazed around us at the outlandish wilderness which
was to be home — our silent driver though familiar with
the place did not open his mouth to explain a thing —
when Lady Edwina dismissed his surliness on the
grounds that he was a known Papist Ann Whittaker retorted that he might have been as horrified by finding
himself in so remote a spot with us as we were at finding
ourselves with him — yet I believe it was more a question
of his belonging and our foreignness — because after all
hadn't the Anglican Earnshaws married into the Roman

Barnetts? — Oliver Barnett and Jack Earnshaw being cousins? —

Does it not strike you as strange that English people are so seldom touched by experience? that whatever happens we remain unchanged? and for all our tenacity in the colonies we have acquired no more in the past hundred years than possession of air and water? — certainly on the afternoon in question I felt it was only because we had lost everything and gained nothing that we were doomed in all honour to stick it out —

We haven't *learnt* much collectively (have we?) which we could not have learned at home — apart from the sentimental value of lost origins —

I squeezed Flora's hand when she took hold of mine because I guessed she dreaded dying in such a barren waste — but now I look back on it I wonder if she foresaw what was to come for the rest of us — the poor thing wept openly when everyone crowded round to lift her out and settle her in a patch of sunshine —

This much I do admit that though I love to chew over a good memory I never had any talent at guessing the future — hence my perpetual New Year resolution to be obedient —

I looked over my shoulder in time to glimpse our guides shaking their shaggy heads while they unpacked the heavy bags — carrying the last items past Louisa who sat gazing ahead at a huddle of little rooftops half-buried in shrubbery and showing no sign of alarm maybe because she needed to concentrate her energies on recovering — or maybe simply because she was a stodgy German potato as Ann used to say —

The Irishman offered Louisa his arm so he wasn't wholly dead to chivalry while my husband took the other side and they led her away to the gate — meanwhile perhaps because the load had been lifted the ponies began bucking at phantoms — the shafts clashing together — but we could not quite make out whether anything else might be the matter until one pony's hoof caught another on the side of the nose with a terrific smack — the Irishman's sulky jerked back and slammed into a tree where it fetched up askew while the frightened animal shook her head and bared her teeth — well this wasn't very important except that when the fellow ambled across to calm the poor thing and lead her away from the others we could see one axle had been damaged — "He might fix it for the time being but it's his father's" Jack Earnshaw explained.

The wheel wobbled.

Mr Moloch watched without interest but you mustn't forget that being a prophet his attention was generally on matters beyond the immediate present — unless the grimness settling in his face was an effect of those nagging aches which went with his touch of lameness — in the meantime madam had shown herself as the type who has never been taught to climb into a brougham let alone how to step down gracefully yet she looked very imposing standing still —

Plainly our drivers regarded Mr Moloch as a charlatan
and were displeased when he waved them off without the
least gesture of hospitality while to us he said as reassur-
ingly as he could "I believe we shall find the house complete with furniture left by the Barnetts" — oh yes those
Barnetts got out with nothing more than the clothes they
wore and the hopes they had of Digby Barnett returning
from the Victorian goldfields a rich man — as well he
might because God moves in strange and contrary ways —
none stranger than to think that even when we first discussed moving inland He must have known Louisa's opera
company was already propping up its pictures of disaster
and hanging a canvas tempest for a backcloth at the Melbourne Theatre Royal while singers gathered to do battle
with the inadequacies of a colonial orchestra and what
this would lead to —

All the colonies went mad over gold in those days —
though it seemed to slip through people's fingers — the
cities spent it on celebrations and entertainments and the
diggers spent it on grog —

We watched our guides set out for home and then pause
far off along the track to rein in their ponies while that
nice Earnshaw man waved us a final goodbye — the Irish
giant kept the rock of indifference turned against us —
probably still sunk in worry over his wobbling wheel —

Being so impatient to inspect the house we did not
immediately unharness the ponies though several ladies
remarked on how nervous they seemed —

I walked apart for a minute or two just to try confronting the enormity and sameness of the bush — saying to myself "We have arrived" but the idea of this as arrival made little sense in such a limbo — the laugh I suddenly let out died on my lips — another of my thoughts had come to me — that the usual picture of Hell is of familiar sins and almost domestic sufferings (fire and pitchforks — bleedings and beatings — very much our own penances on a larger scale) whereas it now seemed more likely that an effective Hell would be to suffer in complete meaninglessness for absolutely no understandable reason — can you imagine? —

I developed this — wasn't it arguable that even the old idea of a Hell constructed from experience might work more painfully in meaningless surroundings? — wouldn't this throw the sinner back among her sins — to live in a world of memories? — and we already knew about that — the anguish —

Lost in thought I suppose I did not bother to listen to the voices behind me or try putting meaning to what they said — syllables completely adrift — weird as utterances from another world (which is what they were) surviving in this trap of repeated shapes and monotonous colour — I believe I wept —

Ponies whinnied — one voice at length broke through to me calling "Look sharp!" — I dashed some blinding tears away to find myself confronted by a horde of demons prancing out from among the trees — a squad of them sidling this way and that and beginning to wail tunelessly — ferocious horrors with arms hung down to their knees — things stuck into them and other things stuck out —

Mr Moloch thundered at us to avert our eyes while he dealt with the menace alone — goaded to a fury he was — having so recently performed the greatest of miracles I suppose he was full as a drum with pride and in common with most men felt an urge to strut — fortunately the demons were not to know what I knew — that under his breath he cursed himself for not carrying a loaded gun — curses being a sure sign of fear — and he rushed up to me at a limp —

Will I ever be free of this problem with —

My breath?

I stood petrified where I was — glancing back only once to where Flora lay helpless in the gateway to see Hester (give her credit) hurry that way in case Flora needed somebody to ward them off but no one knew I myself needed special protection for the sake of my unborn child — more perhaps than a dying woman —

So along came these ugly demons in all sizes from huge to tremendous confronted by puny little Mr Moloch making good his humiliation at not being able to drive a cart by rolling up his shirtsleeves bunching his fists and dancing about as he had been taught in the slums while Lady Edwina called "Come come!" from where she yanked at the snaffle of her frightened pony which had not yet been tethered and was crabbing with its buggy into a ditch but nobody took the least notice of her —

I was amazed to see — behind vicious masks watching

the prophet skip unevenly this way and that — eyes full of good humour and eyes full of fear — while it was my husband who gave a desperate shout like the sort of noise you'd expect only a dog to make —

As for the fact that he did begin to carry a gun after suffering this fright — well we were to find out the consequences of *that* later on!

Intense light and shadow swirled round us as gusts of wind crowded among the trees and dashed against my skirts and sent massive chunks of sky flying at my head while I caught at my husband's sleeve to restrain him — he wrenched it free and flung a few words at me so that I stood dazed and bewildered trying to grasp the meaning of what he said — "The grisly wife as always!" —

Was this me? Was I in the way? —

I knew by the stab in my heart at his familiar word "grisly" — he and his opera singer had coined this name together — no use excusing his crudity on the grounds that those closest to Jesus were fishermen and carpenters — not to mention a wild man in the person of John the Baptist — I believe I felt a surge of hope when the demons responded by aiming spears at him — might they achieve what the shipwreck had not? —

They jabbered and waggled their snouts and bared sharp teeth and shuffled webbed wings — not at all the type of congregation Mr Moloch was used to at the Methodist meeting houses in Cleeve Cloud or Chipping Sodbury — "What do you mean — the *grisly wife?*" I shrieked —

anger lifting me beyond fear — like a hero — "In the Lord's name" he roared as he marched right up to them "get thee behind me!" and actually laughed (which sent shivers through me) sounding like some demented being very much bigger than Muley Moloch —

So this was to be the future! this was to be our home which we would make decent enough for the Visitor — the returning Christ — oh yes that was the idea and nothing less — to make ourselves worthy as hosts for the Second Coming in this appalling hole with the peaks of rude shingle rooftops already announcing what squalor we should expect — not to mention the scatter of battered cans and smashed bottles littering the place and scraps of paper blown in under the bushes or the torn shreds of coloured cotton snagged in the branches or the lingering stench of unsanitary living — I drifted into a chasm of self-pity —

I did not care whether I lived or died so I turned my back on the danger and there before me I observed a huddle of women in neat dark clothes — some with cashmere mantles others with pinched waists and lace revers — their bonnets cupping faces wide with horror and eyes so shocked God knows what they thought they were witnessing — whether insects as big as horses or birds with teeth or giant eels coiling through the treetops — and over by the gate where Hester crouched I saw Flora's head on the mattress wag from side to side as they whispered together —

"Come to me Charlotte" Elizabeth Eyre called and took her hand —

What about my baby — I wanted to shout — but all I could manage was to shout after Mr Moloch "If they bite your face off you will be no further use to the Almighty or to me either!" and then my heart emptied of blood at a piercing note which was not a scream but had the pitch of a scream and lodged in the ear as vibrant and pinching as a clever kind of torture and saw Louisa Theuerkauf having shaken off her exhaustion assembling her vast bulk to march forward — impassive like the ivory statue she had seemed to be when washed up dead by the ocean — she took one mechanical step at a time carrying her bosom prominently and her manly shoulders squared and her face nothing more than a frame for the cavity of a gaping mouth — her fair hair ballooning round the whole arrangement while with head well back she uttered this superhuman (what did I decide it was?) top D or top E flat —

Well the demons might have encountered the like of the prophet but they reckoned without Louisa — their hair stood on end between the clumps of feathers and bloody bird-gizzards they decorated it with and they scattered — all but one — tails and appendages flapping and the animal pelts slipping crooked across their shoulders they scuttered and dodged away among the forest trees with weapons rattling —

You should bear in mind that it was I who first introduced the idea that wherever our mission might be we

must make it a decent enough place for the Lord — my
husband and I had been walking back along a Gloucestershire lane with hawthorn bushes at either side and
enjoying the buoyancy of his latest successful sermon —
he had taken up a stick from the grassy bank and broken
it to a convenient length — so he began to invent our
future beginning with a group of select disciples to follow
the true path — perhaps in secret — "However" I said
"my dear man" relishing my role as an adult "the Visitor
will need to recognize how decent it is" — which led to
the question of location because how would *our* decent
place be found in England for example when England
despite its corruption was still so full of the wrong decent
places? —

So to the mission in the hills —

This then was to become the decent place — here
among jungle demons — the very improbability would
offer our best guarantee of being found by the Messiah —
this rustic slum with its first candidate martyr already
laid out at the gate to gasp in extremity while her forehead
was bathed by the most evil of women dipping handkerchiefs in water — and I (as author of the journey) discovered I had already become the victim of a private jibe
enjoyed by my husband and the opera singer who might
very well disqualify us from our purpose by making a
mockery of decency —

The only person I could bear to speak to was Flora
because Flora would soon be dead —

She was all smiles as she whispered that she had not

once coughed since we unloaded her — I felt terrible and I believe I did have a premonition then of some dire tragedy awaiting the rest of us — perhaps aided by Hester — Hester who stood back a little and stared down at me as she asked whether I felt perfectly well and only released me from her enquiry when Martha turned to us to report that the demons had entirely disappeared and to hope very loudly that there were solid locks on all the doors —

Mr Moloch strode back taking longer steps than were natural because plainly he expected credit for the rout — and it must be admitted that Lady Edwina was our sole casualty — her pony had forced the four-wheeler right into a ditch pulling her so violently down the bank she lost her grip on the bridle and being chiefly angry with herself did not stint in her outburst against Louisa "That was a damned fool thing to do!" — she was raging I can tell you from the ignominy of her muddy hole — though true to character she immediately recovered her spirits and called up "But effective!" —

If only to prick Mr Moloch's complacency I too complimented the opera person "How nice that your talent survived after all you have been through" I said but she wasn't to be provoked into listening to any wife (grisly or otherwise) because the world was going to consist of no one else but herself and the prophet who was all for explaining the demons' defeat along the lines of an answer he had from God but the satisfaction gathering and spreading around Louisa to poison the very air we breathed made plain that she knew otherwise —

And soon enough she was to find her speaking voice too because we overheard her cajoling him saying *"Herr Doktor Moloch Muley mein liebschen* such a saint is born in a thousand years exactly only once!"* —

We knew enough German because we sang lieder —

Actually when it comes to the point Louisa was quite a famous opera singer though still very young and discovered by Richard Wagner (he is a modern composer so you will probably not have heard of him) a controversial individual who took her up and she sang in his opera though I have no other authority than herself — she toured to Melbourne and the goldfields to sing the same part and this could be checked because Mr Moloch showed us the Ballarat programme adorned with a Romantic etching of cliffs where storm clouds shot zigzag lightning at a ship carrying the lone figure of its captain wrestling with the wheel —

He confessed he had attended her performance as a celebration after registering our title to the land — which I suppose means little more than that he was starved of entertainment despite having more than enough women waiting at home to dance attendance on him — and yet how had he dared? — he must have felt a fearful dread in his soul knowing he trod forbidden ground — especially as he later recounted the story of two people who had been trampled to death when crowding up

the very corridor he himself had used only minutes
earlier —

Apparently Mr Moloch waylaid her at the stage door
and made her feel so important she determined this was
the way things were going to remain (wife or no wife —
mission or no mission — wilderness or no wilderness) so
please don't imagine I am failing to face the truth just
because I can talk cheerfully and because I have only two
eyes like anybody else —

This is not to gainsay his claim that he *is* the prophet
or to deny his gift and I might have done far worse in
life even without taking the adventure into account —
the point is that years would pass before the truth dawned
on me — those demons were sent when we needed
them — and Louisa likewise —

Our whole life being such an adventure seldom anything lasted long enough to be dull — even the sturdiest
trees had their tops constantly raked by the speed of earth
turning on its axis to tip out a rainbow of parrot wings
and cast down a puzzle of sunshine on hillsides simply
alive with lizards — even on the way in through the gate
wild orchids drooped to touch one's head with stale fleshy
petals and in the garden shadows leapt around brandishing
clubs — all sorts of surprises —

We decided to embrace the fact of those filthy huts
when we saw them despite having paid good shekels —
the more primitive the better we said bravely — cant I'm
afraid — pure cant! —

I could not understand why my husband was so often to be found plunged in a brown study — yet again and again when I went to him he defeated me with a new considerateness which betrayed the fact that he did not love me — and whereas I had once been at fault for just about everything which went wrong including the weather he now began sharing the blame among the others (I felt increasingly baffled that he had ever married me in such haste) so as usual I was caught standing still while the world rushed by! do you see where this is leading?

May I freshen your cup?

Yes well I suppose you find it inconceivable that such a trivial thing as an oblique and unfinished remark overheard in a grocer's shop might goad me to insist on quitting the coast at such risk — but this is precisely the nature of respectability because naturally one would rather die than look foolish —

As I have said — if I am to answer your questions I need to go right back to the beginning and tell you everything — which I am willing to do — so long as I can get the picture clear —

Our first experience of the huts was unforgettable banging open doors and recoiling from the filth of stale rags and putrefying kitchen waste — I swore to remember each painful detail beginning with Louisa taking it upon herself to decree "The kitchen shall be kept clean here for I am angry against dirt!" (though I simply cannot begin to describe what we were to think later when we saw the way she washed herself!) another thing — yes she turned her attention to the two dwelling huts and selected the larger — herding us in — "That is the place for everybodies" she decided as she turned about and marched back to stand in the doorway blocking out the day — she challenged us with her pale eyes of a brine-pickled herring which neither blinked nor flinched —

Would you believe that I still did not take her meaning until we returned to the smaller hut — the original house — boasting curtains at the window with a border of handworked lace — she declared "*Ja!*" like an explorer who comes through a desert to the shores of an inland sea "this will be for Herr Moloch to sleep" she measured the inner of the two rooms with arms spread wide while we tried peering past her "here his bed is" she blocked it in with a chopping motion of the hands "here he himself washes" she blocked that in "here he writes and here on the floor he prays" she then swung round to address the outer room where we were gathered "here" she announced with finality "he sits for his pleases" she blocked in another oblong article "here the couch is where I sleep" and she concluded such arrangements satisfactorily by bringing her big sticky hands together like a gun shot —

Lady Edwina's opinion was that we should find her a suitable butcher and marry her off without delay —

For my part I can tell you I was going to murder Louisa — I was going to strangle her fat neck or poke

her eyes out or pour arsenic down her throat or push her
into the fire or drown her in mud or tie her to a stake for
ants to eat the flesh off her bones or at very least offer
her as a sacrifice to the demons to keep them occupied
with good works — I was ready to forsake the chosen few
and join the damned — my pregnancy gave me the courage and I thought I had strength for anything —

But I was not strong enough for what I encountered
that very first evening as the sun was going down —

I had been assigned the kitchen to clean and I had
broken another cup of Edwina's precious tea set — I went
outside to collect my wits — well Mr Moloch having
raked together some scattered leaves and twigs had set
them alight — the ladies sweeping and scrubbing our
quarters emerged now and again to feed the fire with bits
of rubbish — I myself would soon contribute my share —
the little kitchen building I might say stood separate from
the rest for safety's sake because sparks from the tin chim-
ney tended to shower the shingle roof so Digby Barnett
had left a clear area of packed earth between — this was
where the fire was —

The point is that I hid my crime of the broken cup —
so you see how vulnerable I suddenly felt in my own
home — and I was looking for a means of disposing of
it — I leaned on the door frame beside a bucket of mouldy
scraps and crumpled boxes for consigning to the flames
when an unpleasant and familiar odour distracted me from
my plans — how can I explain? — I want you to smell

what I smelt — I want you to see what I saw there — out in the yard the fire burned energetically with a heap of dry branches crackling in the flames and a column of smoke with a fancy head to it blossoming in among the tall straight trees —

We were making progress —

Ann Whittaker could be heard from across the way softly singing a hymn while she sat at the table working with the sewing machine which I heard start and stop and start and stop — otherwise the place seemed suddenly deserted (I later learned that most of the Stars had gone off scouting for wood) though a couple could be seen drawing water down near a vegetable patch the Barnetts had once dug but then with their characteristic sloth let run wild — they drew small pails from the stream for emptying into a bigger container — Hester Partington and Lavinia Dudgeon — Lavinia had once been in an asylum you know — then they stooped together to lift the large pail using a pole thrust through its handle — they approached in a wobbling awkward way and even at a distance I saw the sides of the pail sheeted in slops as bright as glass —

Let me get my breath a moment.

This old trouble!

The obnoxious odour turned out to be common enough — the tart stench of burning cotton — cotton which Louisa Theuerkauf poked into the flames while presenting a view of her mannish back with the straps of a borrowed apron cut tightly across it —

She had a way of being busy without moving much —

You could almost imagine the whole fire spouted from her stick as she stirred a smoking mess of something white and black-edged which flopped about and practically put the show out altogether like the turning wing of a dead white eagle — she prodded it and lifted it to let a draught revive the flames — this absorption was unlike her usual composure — I found myself tantalized until I hit on the appropriate word — she was *enjoying* herself —

The scorched rumplings of stuff caught and a renewed gout of evil smoke thickened till I thought I would be sick on the spot but what was there to complain against? and nohow could I demand she stop what she was doing without speaking to her! so I made a great matter of fetching a tablecloth I had rinsed and I hung it out letting the fabric slap damp and cool against my cheek —

The water-carriers drew near — the wicked Hester calling cheerfully "Pooh pooh pooh!" as they crossed towards me and staggered up the steps to my clean kitchen — while I took root by the clothesline with the crinkled cloth faintly steaming like an animal skin and refusing to hang square — "The floor's not dry!" I warned as they put their pail down on the top step and propped their pole against the doorpost — leaving a flat bright world of light to tilt and rock on the water's surface they set off to tackle another chore —

"Buck up Louisa!" Hester called over her shoulder —

I knew I was screwing up courage to face what was happening and yet I had to be prompted by hearing my

husband's boots on the verandah of the private quarters
(this house we are in right now) and seeing him emerge
carrying a bundle of cotton clothes tucked under his arm
as if he hoped he would not be recognized — when at
last Louisa herself looked up she reached out to take the
bundle and straightway flung it on the fire —

They stood side by side to watch it burn while the
flames wilted under the extra burden and she coaxed them
back with her stick —

So far they had not noticed me but now I did not care
if they did and I rushed over to the dormitory to burst
in on Ann who was serenely singing above the whir of
the sewing machine " — for virgin souls laid up on high
And ready keep her lamp at night To hail the Bridegroom
drawing nigh And surely Thou at last didst come To end
the sorrows of Thy bride And bear her to Thy peaceful
home With Thee forever to abide" — the sewing machine
was said to have cost Lady Edwina ten pounds — Ann
was feeding a seam through while the needle stabbed and
stabbed it at a terrible rate — she glanced up ready to
scold me but then half rose with concern at what she
saw — I am sure she had no intention of letting me see
the full length of the new garment but on recovering her
wits she gathered it swiftly and whisked the hem up off
the floor —

This garment was a man's nightshirt and she reached
out to take me by the hand as one might offer to protect
a small child (the poor poppet) from unnecessary

fears "He needs a fresh one" she explained "now the others are to be burnt" —

You see how good I am? you see how I can look the fact in the face? how I can tell you about even the awful things? — how the nightshirts he had worn in bed with me were treated as contaminated?

I did not show myself at dinner — nor did I move from the dormitory so that by evening when the others came in to prepare for bed I was already there — with no mind to deliver my full feelings as to the treatment I was suffering — the door was shut and padlocked on the outside by our jailer — we had to cope packed into that squalid little shanty with scant room to move among so many bodies jostling in a rustle of crinolines and yet instead of moaning against our discomfort the rest tattled and made the most of it by commenting on that woman and her surviving voice — "The most absolute dragon!" Lady Edwina said to help me out of my difficulty — besides gossiping about all manner of interests from news of modern scientific opinion that a person might die and yet leave some isolated part of them still palpitating (such as a live heart in a dead body or a live hand by itself) to niceties of description concerning a drowned person's jellied eyes and seaweed lips or to marvels such as feet being so saturated they squidged a trail of colourless blood or to persons giving off the whiff of a bedraggled turkey in consequence of not washing —

Meanwhile hairbrushes whacked at loosened tresses and

teeth glimmered and stays whipped and pretty noses grew sinister so I was released from my knots to loll about and dream how I would one day show myself for the brilliant person I kept hidden — then I well remember Whatsaname (this wretched absentmindedness of mine! there are times when I don't know how I shall remember to take the next breath!) well anyway it doesn't matter.

Flora began coughing — did I say? —

In England and on the voyage out I had been protected from overhearing their spite because I was the butt of it but now they included me so at last I belonged.

I felt I might burst if I did not let out the secret filling me with terror and unthinkable power — well you must bear in mind what a torment it was to my conscience and my decency because I felt all the more violated for being so totally innocent and so totally helpless —

The sheer anger of mortification is a thing more easily conveyed by a person's eyes than —

Mr Moloch's mission was exclusively for the female sex with himself the only male on the place — so it was small wonder we had stared at those fleeing demons and especially the one hesitating long enough for me to see he was a callow ogre with a boy's mouth and sinews trembling under polished skin — wings of woody growths flapped on his back when he also fled away and I held him captured in my mind — absolutely complete — his wonderment and his runner's body —

Poor Mr Moloch never looked like that though I am

sure none of us would have dared think of him in those days as poor anything —

How life changes other people and yet leaves oneself untouched (are we never prepared?) — leaves one lumbered with the useless baggage of security property etiquette etcetera — leaves one lumbered with memories — in this case with the sight of ladies bustling about though their bodices were unfastened and myself for the first time placing my boots on the rack among theirs while we agreed in concert to condemn that Jezebel who had lived the sinful life of the stage —

Beyond question we believed in Mr Moloch and his inspiration when it came to explaining the nature of the Holy Ghost yet we doubted he understood the first thing about Louisa Theuerkauf and let me tell you it hit me like a thunderclap that therefore he might understand nothing whatsoever about us either — this hurt because the plain truth was that we followed him like martyrs so even if he had wanted somebody *killed* I suppose we would have dispatched the deed without a second thought and simply to reassure him —

So I came to belong among the Hidden Stars in a dormitory smelling of undergarments when a voice shrieked "Listen!" and we froze but Flora Gilchrist's laboured breathing drowned out anything else that might have been heard — we simply exchanged glances by the fitful lamplight —

You could picture us as fragments of Mr Moloch's single

creation crowding the tiny dormitory so that the room became nothing but a box crammed with parts such as one lady's dimpled elbow joined to another lady's rounded shoulder and hands of several sizes making nearby gestures while others fluttered in the distance to touch locks of red hair or brown where someone's malicious sneer was returned and someone else's fawning eye faltered with alarm — you should imagine us sharing all eighteen legs and ten torsos and you should imagine us sprouting old creaky flaps of skin among young breasts — imagine a nest of restless passions and a rack of used air — because we were the one beast Jealousy with a bristly mole on a jaw otherwise hidden from view and two knobs of a spine where someone bent to unlace her boot unaware that her straight leg might show swollen veins behind the knee or that the person she half-obscured might be polishing a set of claws or that twin heart-hairlines side by side might suggest duplicity or the hollow at the base of a throat might echo an empty mouth above it from which sobs would soon escape —

The thrill of a bullet could hardly have been more rivetting than that sudden rigid silence revealing us as degraded by an appetite we never confessed to (so that any quality or quirk which might have saved us by re-covering the identity of Lavinia or Elizabeth Eyre or Elizabeth Canning had been lost) but I believe we gloried in this bestiality because if we could not be avenged on Mr Moloch we would be avenged on ourselves —

Now will anyone kindly tell me what other choice was offered us — being only human? — and whether in my place they could have told a single soul about their agony or about the even stranger satisfaction soothing me like a caress and making my skin tingle? —

Eventually the silence in the dormitory broke into titters and a flurry of petticoats — such simpletons we were that I believe most of us assumed our laughter did less harm to Louisa and Mr Moloch than to ourselves — though there was little call to indulge in merriment apart from wounding them by forcing them to hear how cheerfully we had settled in.

I would rather you did not sit with your back to the window because I cannot see your face now the daylight is so dazzling out there.

The point being that Ann Whittaker stared and stared at me as I stood revealed in my camisole so I saw (by the way her eyes darted from side to side to check if anybody else noticed what she had noticed) that she knew my secret — the bond between us became in that instant a tremendous conspiracy and I immediately sat down — piling a loose garment on my lap —

Would I be able to speak to her of my fears and my bafflement? could she perhaps help prove I was mistaken — that the sparking flashes in my blood might be no more than symptoms of hysteria and probably a belated consequence of my recovery from the consumption? — when I imagined how peremptorily my parents (in her position) would judge and disown me I felt so grateful to Ann I lost my voice and could offer her no more than a pleading look —

Excuse me a moment.

Come to think of it one might say that our unseemly laughter had been let loose by the corrupting air of this colony where nothing matters yet if Mr Moloch had presented himself in the doorway at that moment we were so well-bred we would have affected ignorance of the least scandal despite the fact that he was shutting the woman away with him — almost certainly we would have asked whether he was comfortable in there while declaring ourselves content with the quarters we had been allotted — if necessary we would have invented pretty lies to account for our boisterousness —

He did present himself too — that was a frightful shock — him in a fury scrabbling at the padlock and then thumping the door so hard he made the wall shudder —

We kept him waiting because our cheeks were still flushed with echoes — meanwhile elbows dimpled again and white arms plunged into dry sleeves to box the starched folds out of them as we made ourselves decent — we also had to face the possibility that we were mistaken in our faith because despite his miracles Mr Moloch showed signs of being only human — perhaps he may not know what he was talking about after all — he certainly risked making a fool of himself hammering for us to invite him into our hut —

You should picture our heads butting out from neck-holes like nothing so much as plain caterpillars who have left it too late to take wing on the butterfly colours they lust for (oh I belonged among the rest already I tell you) with the dim lantern light sputtering because we had used up all the available air in our gladness that I had fallen from my high place —

How odd — I was about to be confronted by my husband as nobody with more right to courteous treatment than a washerwoman — which accounts for the ladies' gruesome interest when they caught my eye — not even my friend Lady Edwina knew the right thing to say to the terrible question of his mute presence in the door frame — when I spoke up —

What's that?

I am told I had gone pale as death and I can recall wanting the earth to swallow me but my voice came colder than Edwina's even at its coldest — just as my words were words one might have taught a foreigner rather than my own "Kindly spare me a minute in private Mr Moloch!" —

Ann collapsed against the cupboard.

I wonder would I have found the courage to confess even then had not my husband led the way back to his room and ushered me in without a word? probably not — but as it was — there in the light of my own lamp which I had chosen for my personal pleasure — Louisa Theuer-

kauf stood up to face the intrusion so I found myself
caught between the two of them and in an eruption of
rash anger launched my attack "I think you should know
I am with child!" and held my breath at the enormity of
what must follow though I did not dare look Mr Moloch
in the face "I have been with child for four months!" —

The lamp burned — flame steady — and my pink
shade cast such gentle light I admired it as if I had never
seen the thing before while Louisa simply cocked her large
head to squint the more shrewdly at me and then cocked
it the other way to gauge my husband's reaction — just
from this I sensed that they had been in each other's
arms — oh yes I knew — as certainly as if I had come
upon them by surprise and seen for myself — I knew —
meanwhile insects screamed into the night —

The dormitory next door stood hushed —

I had indulged my madness and I tried to read Mr
Moloch's reaction in the mirror of Louisa's next move but
I could make no sense of it because she came up to touch
me for the very first time — a most unexpected thing —
"The child lies quiet" she reported with her possessive
hand flat on my tummy "like an old man already" — by
her stiff manner of speaking I guessed her latest twist of
cruelty — now she was hatching a scheme to rob me of
my son at the moment of birth — to bring him up as
her own because she was not content with having robbed
me of my husband —

I pulled away — covered my face with my hands —

poor mite with the spirit so easily knocked out of me and no premonition that one day it would be left to Louisa to restore my sense of humour my right to be angry —

I was in the grip of the unknown so no wonder I fell to my knees quite incapable of further speech while all my rehearsed explanations crowded at once into my throat and choked me so what else should I expect but that he would cast me out and disown my unnatural baby? —

Mr Moloch asked "Is this the sign we have been waiting for?" and asked it in the tenderest manner imaginable — you may guess my amazement — and he knelt beside me as he added "the greatest miracle of all?" — he smiled his gallery of teeth —

Had I won him back at the very moment I thought I must lose him forever? and had the Devil prodded me to speak for no other reason? and did the Devil or something of the same ilk guide Louisa in her turn —

There was a moment during which her stolid face underwent the changes of a developing idea — so that at first I expected her to scream at me — next I expected her to scream at him — then she mustered her professional training as she met my defiant gaze — there was only a hint of haste — only the very slightest edge of hardness to her tone to show how she managed it as she said "Our divine child!" — yet she knew she had betrayed herself.

I could not leave well alone!

What did I do but tempt fate by pestering my husband to continually assure me that his mind was quite at ease about the baby? I forced him to listen again and again to my fierce dogged insistence that I did not know what had happened to me —

To give him credit he became so very handsome during these harangues that I almost always broke down and begged him to tell me what it meant — or to condemn me — yet I knew when I encountered no resistance that perhaps I just wanted to have him to myself and possess him and swallow him whole — crude manners and all — don't worry about his stuck-out ears because even at our wedding he had been the radiant one while I remained confused and conceited and suffered two pimples on my chin besides a soggy nose — well at sixteen years I was nowhere near ready to address the question of whether light bounces back off objects rather than spearing through a shell of appearances to be lodged within or whether that rock at the mouth of Christ's tomb might have been blasted away by light rather than manually and clumsily rolled aside — but this is to tempt us into a discussion of theology —

Meanwhile the life of the mission took on an ecstatic turn with every routine a celebration of the coming child — we began shortly after dawn each morning sweeping and scouring the huts and tucking our bed-clothes tight as boards over the mattresses — every stick of furniture had to be waxed till it squeaked and the walls whitewashed — we starched our blouses and dressed our hair while listening to extracts from the Holy Scriptures — then filled with joy we hastened into the yard for hymns before breakfast — our breath steaming in cold weather — this outdoor singing lifted us free from all the shackles of uncertainty —

Those years in England when we had not been living in the spirit came to seem more like a previous life than an earlier period of this one (which incidentally helped us have compassion for our parents' faults and let go many foolish attachments once thought to be friendships) though Lavinia who feared her family particularly welcomed the chance to hold them in disdain and forgive them with the highest motives —

We threw our energy into civilizing tasks — we were translated as Shakespeare would say — no longer the same people — we taught the prophet to read and write —

As for Mr Moloch his civilizing task was to mark out a lawn and begin pitting himself against a tangle of waist-high weeds — you know I could never bring myself to call him "Moloch" though in moments of tenderness I have many times called him "John" which was his given name —

I might say he'd always had a poor opinion of families — and resented mine — the one thing he dreaded most was that we might walk out so he liked to be certain we had nowhere to go — which also explains why he discouraged us from reminiscing about our childhood — and why he put a ban on letters home and confiscated any that came in —

Occasionally I found him chuckling over those letters because he could have quite a sense of humour provided you tickled the right spot and once in a while he would look up at me and pass me a page with portions snipped out — jagged scissor cuts chopping short a dozen lines here and half a dozen there — from time to time I would accept one such broken-backed object to spread it on the table recognizing the hand and seeing my own name with the end snipped off and I'd stare at a frightful hole in which calamities might have been reported (or love confessed — who knows?) while he got up from his chair scrumpling the censored bits into a ball and kneeling down to burn them in the grate — on other mail days he might burn the entire bundle —

But who is to say he was wrong or that we were in a

position to judge for ourselves? in those days before Louisa made her mark we were grateful for what we received — we accepted that an offending passage may simply have seemed to us like town gossip when in fact insidious ideas were slipping past our guard disguised as comic doings of a distant cousin — or whoever — it is certainly not true that my husband did such things in secret —

We had already made our commitment to Jesus and once the baby arrived we knew this would cost us a great many more contacts — so having previously given our families into his hands we began to be relieved — if you like — that he found them guilty enough to hack their messages up and that he refused to allow us to send them our news —

For the same reason Christmas was forbidden at the mission — our once-a-year greetings had to be sent at Easter instead — this we did seated together around the big kitchen table each holding in mind a different face — and I confess we were torn — many a secret tear being mopped or dashed aside — which is odd when you consider that we had all been desperately unhappy back there — I suppose it was our perversity — rebelling against the idea that the main function of these Easter greetings anyway was to prevent some nosey relative posting us as missing persons and setting the British authorities on to our leader —

I did once receive a whole letter with absolutely nothing cut out of it — the chill of apprehension! — though curiously it was a letter full of rejoicing at Father's elevation to dean and of course I too felt gratified for him (as well as grateful to the censor) because of all things I believed being dean might bring my parents some contentment at last — and some proof that I had not permanently blighted Father's reputation.

The months and weeks ticked by in precious minutes — we were all so breathless with waiting that we never let the waiting alone — meanwhile my baby became quieter and quieter until he lay still in the womb whether because of the anxiety around me or not I can't say — imagine my terrors! — yet he was not dead because he grew steadily larger and weighed me down at a time when already I had the gravest difficulty managing my own weight — the mirror confronted me with the frail fleeting papery mask of a stranger disturbingly like I used to be and yet even more disturbingly unlike I used to be —

So — not only did Louisa claim to be the latest of Christ's converts to be raised from the dead but claimed a place in my most personal affairs by referring to the baby as "*our* divine child" — in addition to which she immediately set about removing Mr Moloch out of his room and advised him to make a bed of hay so he could sleep with the animals in the barn while she remained faithfully where she was on her selfsame couch with new duties — from then on I had the extra burden of her watchfulness —

My husband took his expulsion remarkably tamely because after all he was (and still is) a devout man well
versed in the Gospels —

But none of this endeared her to me or lessened my
hatred for her pallid skin and fluffed-up hair and her large
gestures — nothing to lessen my hatred for her froggy
fingers with suckers or her huge feet and solid ankles or
the effort she made to control her cold assessing stare and
private little smiles or her manner of superior simplicity
which one could easily call the vast spaciousness of the
woman's ignorance — whereas Muley Moloch welcomed
his discomfort which seemed to rouse his spirits until he
positively revelled in humiliation and waxed so gloriously
eloquent that I never entertained the least suspicion of
his sincerity in caring for me and the child.

I was installed in comfort and the worst guilts were
behind me — like those frightful weeks which had cul-
minated in the shipwreck — I was one of the rare ones
to recover from the consumption — indeed the only one
among those who caught it at our mission — Dr von
Lossberg tells me this was because I had the luck to have
contracted it when I was young — but my husband has
lately begun citing my recovery as another of his quiet
miracles — I don't know — and whatever anyone says
now I had mixed feelings then — suffering the sharpest
anxiety that my pregnancy could still be used against me
and that my good fortune could end in punishment —

suffering the insidious fears of an invaded body anony-
mously possessed — who had done this? who? who? —
suffering because I did not know and because I had no
idea where to look for the answer — being left with nothing but a constant smothered scream of disgust — the
wreckage of my trust — a frantic fruitless effort to grasp
at thin air — although well on my way to recovery from
the illness and lying in state in the most private of sanc-
tuaries gazing up at the moon as I had once gazed so long
ago when Dora lay likewise awake on the next bed I was
the prisoner of self-interrogation — in a ferment of perpetual wariness about the least noise — the place was full
of practised eavesdroppers who might be able to read
thoughts by now —

This was my condition when the Voice spoke to me!

I should explain that I am forever stopping in the
middle of doing something to listen inwardly because I
feel an essential word about to come — but this was
different —

Don't ask what the Voice sounded like because although
it has since visited me many times this is a question I
cannot answer to my own satisfaction except to say that
it speaks without actual words (I have to find words for
it afterwards) — as to the tone of what I hear it is a kind
of warmth — certainly less than the communications Mr
Moloch used to have when he told us God came to him
as a well-set-up man with the finest manners imaginable
and friendly gestures —

My Voice gave no messages suggesting those might be the last days of Earth nor calls to bind Satan — it just reassured me with feeling "You may depend upon it that the Lord is coming!" while moonlight around my pillow broke into the most beautiful scene imaginable of a hundred fluttering angels' wings — the softest caress of something joyful —

Next morning Louisa came and sat on my mattress to confide in me — she *had* entertained the ambition of a spiritual marriage with my husband believing he gave her good warrant — but now she repented because during the night she had been shown how wicked this was in the event of my carrying the miraculous infant and so forth —

Instead of slapping her face soundly I admit I softened as an exhausted child aching to be cradled in somebody's arms — at least to discover what that would be like —

Louisa talked until she brought herself to confess that she first came to dedicate her life because she had never been able to contemplate allowing any man the least liberty — then her quest began for a Husband of the Soul who would be no more to her carnally speaking than a being from another world if such a thing might be imagined —

It would appear that the Almighty intended preserving her purity for my service and support —

But this was not what dazzled me with amazement —

What dazzled me and confused me was how painlessly

the crisis resolved itself — how readily my dear husband
had heard me without once doubting my word though
the matter of it was strange indeed — I arose feeling
wonderfully refreshed and determined upon universal forgiveness when I glimpsed a fleeting dark body emerge
from our larder to vanish in the jungle — I nearly cried
out but caught myself in time to realize that because of
what the Voice told me I must take special care of the
local demons who were neither more nor less than lost
souls — God delights in forgiveness —

I dreamed that I myself might run away! — though
naturally I told no one — not even my dearest Ann who
behaved like a cross but loving mother to me —

"Scholars are writing how Saint Joseph made eighty
when Jesus was born" Louisa reminded me — also that
Joseph is not mentioned as being present for the actual
delivery of the Christ child in either Gospel dealing with
the virgin birth "however" she added significantly "Mary
was not lonely by herself already — no — because she
had with her a lady — yes — a lady she called her cousin" —

Louisa was so filled with jubilation she grew inex-
haustible — she would declare God's glory among the
heathen she would reproach and scorn whosoever deserved
to be scorned she would rejoice as a bride rejoiceth over
a bridegroom and set up the tabernacle of Moloch —
the tabernacle of witness in the wilderness as required in
the Acts of the Apostles — with her own hands she must

erect the chapel immediately which she would consecrate to our coming child —

No one knew how to plan a building but Elizabeth Eyre was willing to try (I might say she drew so beautifully her uncle had once sent her drawings for publication to a firm in the Haymarket) and produced a sketch for Gordon Pringle to check — the elder Gordon Pringle of Cuttajo who had already approached Mr Moloch to ask whether we allowed new people to join the mission or attend our services — because accepting neighbourly advice on the matter of the chapel was one way of rebuffing the man without offence — allowing him to have some part in putting up the building he was to be excluded from and at the same time securing help at less than the ten shillings a day being asked by workmen.

Oh you may laugh young Arrell but isn't this exactly the kind of thing going on all around us now with talk of Federation — insisting on boundaries?

The chapel was built and the prophet named it the Ladies' Chapel because he had told us we must keep the real dedication secret in case some Herod might have the boy murdered (some Sir Hercules Robinson or who you will — though come to think of it Sir Hercules was not yet in power was he?) —

The hardest thing over the years was keeping the secret from the boy himself to give him a chance of growing without vanity and being open to learning his father's trade while living the same simple life Jesus had lived — but more of this in due course —

Despite Ann's forebodings we borrowed some convicts for the job of stripping bark slabs from the trees — each sheet had to be soaked and flattened ready for nailing to the frame — you seldom see a job done that way these days — the same for the roof except that we also had to make a grid of lashed poles for laying on top to save it being blown off —

The convict builders protested against the lack of a window on the grounds of civilized precedent but Mr Pringle said not a word — he knew our services were private now — so the chapel was completed and once the door closed we were left with only a frail net of light glancing in through the cracks and joins above and around us which allowed us each to make out other praying silhouettes —

That was the coldest place in winter —

You may imagine us in our simple clothes — having long since given up fine fabrics — emerging from the dormitory in pairs to walk across the yard holding our breath as if about to plunge into cold water — our fingers made soft and insensitive by gloves clutched tiny Bibles with bone covers and brass hasps — as we filed in to establish our solitude among others in solitude while the door swung to behind us and Muley Moloch's shape trod to the front where he began preaching one of those fierce inspired sermons beginning with "Except ye see signs and wonders ye will not believe" or with "Ye shall be witness unto me even unto the uttermost part of the earth and so forth" with the words flashing like drawn swords to cleave us asunder — after which we would hasten to the table for our morsel of bread and our sip of wine — kneeling while the prophet performed the ceremony — then returning to our pews with glad hearts knowing that once outside we would burst into song with "What if death my sleep invade Shall I be of death afraid? Whilst encircled by Thine arm Death may strike but cannot harm!"

I see your point but when I say we knelt in seclusion this was a seclusion made possible by knowing we knelt *together* because surely society is necessary to seclusion if the seclusion is to be neither desolate nor threatening? and since many of us were at one stage or another of the illness we were grateful to conceal the difficulty we had breathing — not to mention the chance of concealing our sunken looks —

Although we sang hymns all day we never sang in chapel — the special appeal of chapel was the silence enveloping us once the prophet had spoken — the healing tranquillity of a sanctuary from punishments — which lasted well after Mr Moloch walked back to the door and out — leaving us with the purity of being women among women.

How can I hope to explain what this meant?

You are a man so perhaps you are not aware of the world being jealously possessed by men or that regardless of how indulgent a man may be he won't let go once he has some little bit of it in his fist and feels he has the right to mock or revile anything not yet in his control.

I mentioned a slim demon flitting away from our pantry and I ought to have added that such raids became common — during our first few months here we often saw these lost souls clustered at the verge of the clearing to mock and laugh us to scorn while we directed the borrowed convict labourers to beat back the forest and dig a new vegetable garden (it was considered especially humorous for one of the ladies to give an order to a man and for him to obey) but eventually the audience shrank and took to shuffling on the spot and retreated under giant ferns — which we accepted as a sign of growing respect until Lady Edwina slapped her thigh and declared that they were able to smell the sickness raging among us —

When coughing spread until virtually the whole mission began to weaken the demons stayed away altogether "They've a nose for death" Edwina confirmed "and it terrifies the poor lost creatures" — tragedies kept happening which were not my doing at all because I was never inclined towards vengefulness and was as much left gasping at the shock as anybody —

Once we finished the chapel the next big job was to dig a freshwater well but by then the first of the convicts had fallen ill too and their owners took them back for fear they might all be lost if they remained — and in any case we had embraced the opportunity to do labouring work during the day which was a strange liberty — then we sat round in the evening discussing my pregnancy which some of our maiden ladies found fascinatingly distasteful — almost all of them being ignorant of whether or not matters were progressing satisfactorily (you may include me also) — indeed had it not been for Martha Sparrow with her experience I believe these discussions would have driven me to a constant panic —

The first sign of life in the womb is a flutter so gentle you think perhaps you might have a touch of wind but then in a flash of awe you recognize the spark of creation and come to hear each little tremor as a word spoken in the blood — Saint John one one — In the beginning was the Word and so forth —

You cannot imagine how far skin will stretch nor how huge a baby feels when you are carrying it around inside — just to lie on one's back becomes desperately uncomfortable in the late stages and throughout the night one is driven to shift from the right to the left side — using both hands clasped around this other life to support it — and by then the flutter has developed to a tyranny of activity so that sleep is impossible while the unseen baby kicks you and sends lightning bolts along your nerves — nausea sets in with the horror of outrage that you are host to a parasite with a will of its own who drains you of strength till you are tortured by cramps and your back aches — not to mention waterbrash rising like acid in your throat each time the heartburn takes your breath away until you begin twisting and turning to escape the inescapable — just to draw breath — just for an instant to throw off the suffocator's pillow — that's the truth —

The pregnant woman also squirms and turns in her heart to find some way of staying as she was but she is bound to be changed because at the deepest level of mystery the new life has already made a monster of her pride (oh yes) — you've no idea — and even the fear you experience can become a weapon for making your husband feel ever more hopelessly excluded from the female power over life —

Meanwhile you suffer humiliating appetites — you have a craving to eat earth and no matter how guiltily you go about digging with your bare hands numb and tingling somebody is sure to catch you at it —

Even so in my case I flourished because I am an optimist and because the more often I am cast down the more surely I raise myself up again —

So my baby growing huge and alien in the womb was a source of power as well as the cause of acute anxiety even while he hooked his little feet round my ribs to give me terrible twinges and I watched one after another of our ladies register creeps at placing her palm there to feel how wilful he was and how independent of me long before he was actually born — not to mention the nauseous business of breasts weeping or the many times I needed to rinse my garments to save others the embarrassment of knowing about my bodily changes —

Where could I turn for advice? —

Regardless of what anyone says pregnancy is tedious and exhausting — only lightened by occasional bursts of inner radiance (but maybe this was because mine was a special child so for others you ought perhaps to discount the radiance) and he *was* a special child —

Louisa managed the whole affair — from caring for my comfort to telling the prophet how he ought to adjust his daily routines and prepare for the role soon to be entrusted to him — he never opposed her which made me suspicious because I knew how hotheaded he could be especially when touched on the raw by any suggestion that lack of education left him less fit to decide what was proper or where wisdom lay — but how about me? — was I supposed to forget the nightshirts she had burnt because they had been contaminated by contact with me?

You see how involved things were and why I grew so very angry?

Meanwhile more ladies fell ill and I was kept from seeing them because the child had to be protected — so for a month I saw only Louisa and Mr Moloch (not even Ann was allowed near though she seemed mercifully immune to consumption) — during this time Elizabeth Eyre who could sing a tenor line down to E and was commonly supposed to have been born without a womb died unexpectedly and then they told me that dear Flora was finally in extremity —

There is no doubt Flora had been a trial to me from the outset when she became the first disciple and right till the end refused to give up her function of converting Mr Moloch's passing remarks into articles of dogma —

What made the news of Flora and Elizabeth worse was a conversation I overheard through my open window.

Lack of breath again.

The other Elizabeth — Elizabeth Canning — and Charlotte were telling Hester Partington how the prophet had explained that it is the animal within us which gets out of control and how Flora had responded by whispering "We want nothing — from anyone" — when Hester cut them short by declaring that the old system should be brought back because someone must be to *blame* for spreading the illness which could not be passed off simply as contagious — it must be faced for what it was and the guilty person punished — even if that guilty person was in a delicate condition! —

Who else could she have meant?

I knew exactly what the punishments would be — picturing myself being once more thrown to the floor for my hair to be pulled — the fear I felt taught me how much I loved my baby because this was a new fear drenching me in coldness and quite unlike the routine trembling I knew from previously falling short of God's standard — the difference was that it roused ferocity in me now — such that I knew I would not be hit without hitting back in defence of my little one — she had made a grave mistake — she was not dealing with the same Catherine Byrne she had so summarily dealt with in years gone by —

and yet the fear still gnawed away at me — my first defence must be to defy the confessional itself —

What a tremendous thing! — leading even to the notion of renouncing rules altogether —

Hester went on to confirm that my child must indeed be a divine child — that is to say "wholly mysterious" — but she questioned whether due weight had been given to Satan's powers or Satan's habit of modelling his wickedness on God's finest flights —

When my friend Lotte interrupted to whisper that they might be overheard and cause distress I wished I had not so often been sarcastic to her — nevertheless Hester knew what she was about and kept them where they were until she had delivered her poison to the last drop — wishing she could be quite *quite* sure the baby was the promised Immanuel and not a changeling who would bring ruin upon the world and confusion among the faithful —

I heaved myself up in bed and although I could not catch them at it I did see into the hut across the yard — a curtain billowed from the open window to bloom with light — such a pregnant fullness and yet so elegant — I was fascinated by that curtain as a beautiful chance event until the instant when it curled slanted and slipped to one side before puffing out again — an instant long enough for my eye to photograph two figures embracing — but not long enough to see who they were —

In a flash the truth inspired me to whisper out loud "So we are in Purgatory!" with Good clearly on one hand

and Evil on the other — with the possibility of ascending directly to Heaven a mere step away from plunging into the bottomless abyss to fall through an eternity of darkness —

The next morning as soon as Louisa had told me they planned to bury Elizabeth Eyre just up there — you see the clearing on that hillside? — a tremendous hubbub broke out in the forest and even the prison of my comfortable little room resounded to the multitude of bellbirds and the screech of crickets —

I was forbidden to attend — what did this mean? —

The din lasted until they had carried the body to the chosen site and planted another pepperina tree to absorb the germs so that the chipping of pickaxes could scarcely be heard from here — nor the scrape of shovels — then mounting above this storm of little sounds came a remote pure voice rising from syllable to syllable holding the vowels until sometimes they rang out and at other times sank before gathering strength again or sinking yet further from a mere expression of human grief to an impersonal lament for the fleeting joys of this world fading to a resignation so profound I wept despite the cruelty swelling my heart because having feared Elizabeth Eyre's unnatural interest in me I rejoiced at being rid of her — and now this melody pierced my heart with knowledge that in death souls may be united —

So music brought me to face my guilt after all and might have tortured my conscience had not Louisa's elegy been echoed by a soft humming chant from among the trees where I saw (and you may be sure I *did* reach the window this time despite my lumpish condition) a dozen demons in full animal splendour of feathers and tall pointed hats made of sticks —

They were briefly there and soon gone but it was evident to me that they knew more about us than we had ever believed possible —

I remained leaning on the rough sill right there — like this — staring out among the tree trunks when a whole tribe of women appeared before me encouraging me with smiles and open hands in no way like demons' hands and there was little doubt they called to me personally because the rest of the Hidden Stars were busy burying the dead — soft gentle female shapes partly naked and partly dressed in left-off oddments they had had from the townsfolk I suppose — how could I be angry at their shamelessness especially as I marvelled (when they walked into a fresh clearing of sunlight) at how the glory of the Lord shone round about them — and saw by their eyes that they were afraid —

Yet the boldest of these females persisted — even coming right up to the wall — and she reached for my fingers on the sill — "If only you knew how terrified I am" I thought "of Hester!" warm soft fingers touched mine "how terrified I am of carrying Satan's changeling instead of God's child!" the creature's gesture was so tentative I knew the Lord God could mean no harm to her or her tribe so I said "I bring you tidings of great joy which shall be to all people" — because these were not demons — they deserved as much pity as ourselves — and when they called me to the door to stroke my arms and lead me away from that place of misery — out where there were no paths nor any sign which the memory might catch hold of as a guide for finding one's way back — I thought I might go —

Though I hesitated — yes hesitated in the doorway — while staring beyond them seeing again that vivid scene of Louisa tending a fire in the yard — of my husband looking on and seeming not to notice the foul smouldering smoke waft round him — of her lifting a shrivelled black skin of a thing from the flames and holding it on the end of her stick while she let out the only laugh we heard from her that month — and a pail full of water as treacherous as mercury left standing on the kitchen verandah for the dazzling blob of light reflected from its surface to waver in the lens of tears at the corner of my eye —

I scarcely knew which way to turn —

Anguished memories flooded my mind with a chaotic jumble of wounding little occasions — I felt as if shattered glass crunched in my hips so although I had wanted to take my boots off and throw them away because Mr Moloch made them for me I could not face the pain of bending down to undo the laces — I wanted him there to see me scratch my cheeks where his kisses were stored — I would willingly have washed my fingers in acid because they knew the feel of him and poked out my eyes for the way they had looked at him just as I would have welcomed devils gnawing my belly until there was nothing left but a hollow of torn meat and would have wanted my skin stripped off with a surgeon's care to be scoured by a man with a steel comb in his hairy hand and immersed next in warm infusions of dog droppings to violate every pore then primed in an oil barrel before being hauled out for stretching drying and buffing so a perfect stranger's finger and thumb might acknowledge that I had my price at least as an article of commerce —

The thin skin of a sentimentalist —

The mourners on the hill surrounded Hester who was doubled up and seemed utterly broken — I know I generally describe her as quite awful really yet sometimes she could be nice and this moment I ought to have been able to feel sympathy but I could not while my own troubles outweighed even death — so I stared at those bonnets and clustered backs gathered around Elizabeth Eyre's grave — until my staring caused Lavinia (I can see her with her hair flatly braided and coiled behind) to turn and look down my way but I was too angry to offer any other gesture before I joined the visitors and set out across the yard unable to feel the ground beneath my feet so perhaps I had learnt Mr Moloch's gift of flight with the slanted morning lifting me along —

There had been no need to come to a decision because I recognized those few seconds as though I knew them already but I didn't give a hoot about poor Flora (the only person apart from Ann never to join in punishing me) who I had been told was in extremity and who had not gone to the burying but lay looking out through the dormitory door watching me accept the firm dark hands of my guides —

I remember a flicker of dappled leaf shade across my shoulders — and as I look back on her now Flora's mouth is twisted with anguish —

I heard Lavinia wail from up at the gravesite and by her tone I knew she was letting go and that when she collected herself sufficiently to blubber a garbled alarm (the dear soft creature) such as "Getting wild — gate — singing — no — free away — " Mr Moloch would bit by bit assemble it correctly as a warning that I was gone — meanwhile I had precious minutes to make my escape — I was out of the clearing and still walking — past the garden then across the footbridge and up the ridge beyond the creek —

We reached a place deep in the forest where little crimson birds darted through the gloom among fern-trees — and furry animals took refuge in the high branches of the upper tier despite the reptiles there — how can I describe the effect? — this was — this was a place of fungus and juicy undergrowth where sap burgeoned amazing crowns of heart-shaped leaves and fan-shaped leaves — whip leaves and spade leaves — as well as an uncanny creeper with masses of tangled stems and tendrils but no leaves at all —

Here the women stopped to touch me and marvel at

my skin and admire my growing child and trace the smooth shape of my fingernails — all of which they checked in the profoundest silence — meeting each other's eyes but never mine — then they harvested berries for me which I dared not taste for fear of poison especially on the baby's behalf — whispers agitated the forest and there came a sudden scurrying of small animals running away from us in every direction — whether the women at that point understood something I did not or whether they simply despaired of pleasing me I cannot say — but all at once they cried out a single word and ran through the undergrowth — I watched their dark shoulders bobbing and the pale soles of their feet —

They absolutely vanished —

I was alone in a place I had not seen before — I never felt so far from the gardens of the Hall or Miss Honeywood's voice cooing at her peacocks or the smell of new leather harnesses in the judge's stables — I began coughing but managed to keep it smothered — helped by the curiously sweet water I scooped from a basin in the rocks — several drips pattered back setting rings fleeing across the still surface — it was then that I heard an approaching wind among treetops and birds chancing a few calls while I imagined the soil being packed in around Elizabeth Eyre's corpse and heaped on top of her — I thought the air smelt of my own approaching death even though I felt full of vigour — perhaps because such peace would be exactly the peace one ought to embrace ready for the final surrender —

I had no fear of it — I only marvelled at the puzzle of how my baby was to survive — as the Chosen of God *must* survive —

The forest had never been so shot through with enormous beams of light nor had the trees ever been so like iron or the sense of strangeness so strange surrounding my death which would be very unlike the maelstrom of icy water from which Mr Moloch saved Louisa Theuerkauf when she appeared as unimportant as a torn rag thrown against the rocks in a daydream —

People used to say that to decide to die — and to make it happen simply by deciding — was the only thing beyond the power of the mind but I refused to believe this because I had discovered the frightful truth that what I felt for Muley Moloch was as near to love as anything I knew and that there was no other reason why I found myself driven to trail after those native women or let them abandon me.

Let me explain a different person inside me.

I was always puzzled that I so seldom wanted what other people wanted — not interested in money or possessions or marriage (to be frank) or even happiness — I was like a creature of some rare species without any likelihood of meeting my soul's companion — which was why I felt so shaken when I read Mr Howitt's account of his search for poor Burke and Wills when lost beyond Mount Hopeless he came upon the hoof marks of a horse! did you ever read his story? and then he saw the horse straying across that biblical wilderness — a lone beast appearing as fabulous there as a unicorn in your garden and the truly amazing fact was that this horse had not survived from Mr Burke's expedition after all because it turned out to have belonged to Charles Sturt sixteen years before! just to think of it makes my face seize up as hard as a mask even now — this lonely creature watching flocks of birds go by when the frost came to the desert and watching them return when the summer returned again and again the passage of so many birds while the lost horse wandered over a desert of Australian stones never setting eyes on another of its own kind —

I dared to consider myself a freak of sorts — so I had less difficulty believing I carried God's child than most women would have faced — for the same reason I cannot say I felt any overwhelming pride — just fear because such intimacy involved me too closely with the source of power —

I know I am always taken for the one with no special skills who will fit in with what is needed — whether as a third player to read through Haydn's London trios or to roll out the pastry while others spice the rabbits and quarter them for baking *en croute* you know or to hold strips of padding straight while the experts begin tacking a length of quilting — or even such humble and essential jobs as checking that the outdoor oven never drops below baking heat —

And yet perhaps I do have special skills which are of a kind beyond the simple uses of housekeeping or the democratic arts — I feel a certain thrusting in me — some unnamed talent ready to rise from the dark and claim recognition — so there is another Catherine Byrne by no means content to remain mute or unnamed.

A brief anecdote — if you have time.

You remember I told you about Judge Honeywood and what happened as soon as he announced my engagement? well when I left the Hall with my parents we were accompanied down the lane by Major McDonald which put a constraint on us so by the time we squeezed out the courtesy of wishing that empty old soldier goodbye and took our separate way my father was ready to explode with fury "A common bootmaker's wife! is this what you are to be Miss? and how did that stuffed dummy — in his silly wig? — be damned to him! — how did he dare — senile as he is?" —

My poor mother offered moderate explanations but he rounded on her "There is no question Mrs Byrne! none! so kindly do not raise your eyes at me!" his face went mauve and bloodless which I associated with frightful things because once before when this happened he had slapped my face so hard I thought my jaw was broken — the point being that despite his show of agitations and convulsions while he stamped along the lane between hedgerows I still managed to amaze us all by speaking up "If Judge Honeywood wishes to test your loyalty because he wants to be sure of getting the best man for the living at Saint Philip's — four hundred pounds a year

Uncle Herbert says — then I do not think the price too high" —

To this very adult speech I added something much more in character and not at all sarcastic "Why should I value myself so greatly?" —

My father boggled at being accused of selling me for the lovely old church with its square tower and melodious bells — but it was unreasonable to expect him to understand that I perfectly accepted his right — nor could he possibly know how determined I was that neither he nor anyone else would prevent me marrying a suitor who could fly —

Why did I begin on this old story?

The point is that I was out in the forest where the native women who had been leading me ran away in fright.

Once I begin to live it all again I can recollect every detail — my desperate state of not knowing whether I was the most blessed of the Faithful or the most damned — this confusion was further complicated by the vivid past invading the present with something hauntingly similar having happened a long time earlier —

I was lost once as a child in the woods near Stroud — it made a terrible mark on me because although I always said I wasn't afraid of anything I *was* afraid of being lost in the woods again — and I was afraid of my father —

It all flooded back when I came to my senses and realized the women who had brought me to this lonely place would not return and that I was a long way out of earshot of the mission — every detail is fixed in mind as fresh as if it were yesterday — moss on the wet rocks where I sit staring into a bubbling stream — fascinated by a sheet of light continuously rippling over hundreds of polished pebbles — engrossed — I jump when a dozen black parrots flap above me shrieking — parrots unsettle me because I still think of them as belonging in cages — I don't really *like* free parrots come to think of it — at least not in the way I like free cuckoos — a cuckoo *has* to be free if you see what I mean otherwise it cannot be understood for what it is — and I understand how delightful robins are in winter or swallows in summer — but I don't understand flocks of parrots going wherever they please — any more than they understand the poor little "she" or what the flapping of her skirt might mean or her shooing hands now she has stood up to climb the bank of the stream —

She does not understand herself because the person *she* sees in her mind's eye is still a child — a bright vulnerable child reduced to a little bag of misery as she strays among the beech trees when no one comes to save her although I have been calling out and sobbing a long time — until I find a path and escape from the dark woods with their green grass to the back fence of a row of houses until I discover a gate which is known to me and push it open and wail for the washerwoman —

The washerwoman has yellow hair in spite of being

older than anybody — she wears it in a pile instead of having a neat parting and rolled plaits — I am glad to see this pile of hair and to see her watching me across her adjustable mangle which she is proud to own because how many other washerwomen have worked hard enough to save for such a luxury?

She has an unhappy smell of yellow soap —

Her eyes are too tired for surprise though she speaks to me in the voice of a person who has never moved from her Gloucestershire hamlet asking after *your dear papa* and *your dear mama* (yet I am also this desperate "she" scrambling over Australian rocks and still lost on the underside of the world where vines snag her clothes and fallen logs trip her as she clambers up the bank from a stream among tussocks slimy and lank — clutching at her tummy for the baby's sake) —

I wish the washerwoman could be my grandmother because when I tell her about the woods I notice her eyes are not too tired for pain and I feel like a different person who is resting her face against a moss-grown tree trunk in the forgotten world of an ancient gully —

Without quite knowing whether it is a question of escaping or returning an urgency drives her on — even as she slips and falls to her knees — which might mean she can never be a mother now (and that her mother — even if still alive — will never be a grandmother either) —

Parrots scream —

The washerwoman pushes both sleeves up to the elbow to show large arms with skin softened like chamois from a lifetime of oily soap and her hands are strong as she heaves a hefty flat-iron off the stove to bang it along the petticoat spread on her board "You must never get your iron caught in the purfling" she explains and points out a lace trim "if I was to tear Mrs Byrne's purfling she might send her work to some other person mightn't she?"

Yes I believe my mother might though I cannot be sure because I don't know my mother too well which is her own fault since she is always so compliant that she takes on the expression of whoever talks to her with the result that she has no expressions of her own unless she is alone and then — as I know from coming upon her at the mirror — she is a bottle full of anger —

"You had any number of caps like this when you was a tiny babe" the washerwoman assures me — picking a baby's bonnet from the pile — her ravaged but plentiful hair flops in the heat of the stove — her kitchen a shimmer of steam from a perpetual kettle on the hob mingled with the smoky vapours of starch — I decide this is my favourite place in all the world —

I will have to wait many years till my mother (grown so oppressed by the invisible bars imprisoning her that she cannot stand this extra bar being set in place by her daughter who might one day run off with a Jew or elope with a bounder) snaps at me "Don't call her Mrs Boulton! she is your grandmama!" so I declare I — for my part —

shall never be anybody's grandmama and then no one can wound me by calling me Mrs Boulton or Mrs Anything for that matter —

This is the scene in her mind's eye as the stumbling young woman clutches her tummy and talks to herself saying there are other women at the mission without a single Boulton among them so why feel ashamed? —

My grandmother's grief is already hard as a stone — I chatter while she irons underwear ready for other people to put on next to their skin — are there poisons which can penetrate the skin? I wonder — and do any of them look like starch?

I have brown hair though I do not consider it as fine as my mother's even though she is too nice to say so and in any case she cannot spare the energy to look at anyone while her husband goes on gazing into space to keep the terrible things in his mind from showing — though in my case now I am safely at home with my unhappiness again I watch him for no other reason than because I want to see what he will do next —

The young woman in the gully is not yet home —

What he does is to come out of his secrecy with a deadly quiet question "Who let off the mousetrap in the larder?" while his nose is pinched white around the nostrils and otherwise his face goes a ghastly mauve colour   "I did" some girl defies him from behind my cup of warm milk with her unsatisfactory hair already brushed and braided ready for bed — and she remembers why it is that she ran away into the woods in the first place —

"Are you starved in this house?" he storms suddenly and comes at her fighting his way through the air to reach her — his black coat opens out like a scarecrow's coat — "Do you need to steal the mouse's share of cheese?"

She wants to laugh which would be more dreadful than anything else and even the maid hurries out into the scullery to begin clattering dishes because he has his hand ready to strike — but this child won't say she did not eat the mouse's cheese nor will she tell of her fright when the machine (snapping shut on a knife she poked at it) might have broken her fingers — on and on he storms "Did you not hear your mother say the mouse got into her cold cottage pie last night?"

"The mouse is God's mouse" this girl shouts to her own alarm —

And now she is in a delirium and cannot disentangle the past and the present — she is on her knees with her skirt soiled and the great trees are swimming upwards around her — she crawls and she remembers how a little old man in a Captain Cook wig pointed one toe like Carlotta Grisi expecting the paltry gewgaw of a buckle to dazzle such a father as hers.

Ambition is a curious urge don't you agree? being as much as to say if I do not surrender my place in life to struggle for a different place (some other person's place) then I will not quite fully live —

I am sure my parents never guessed how soon Mr Moloch would show himself as curiously ordinary considering my expectation of daily miracles and ourselves being swept along by crowds of adoring disciples — long before we set sail I believe I knew the worst though nothing could have persuaded me to admit it — then at Chipping Sodbury the oddest little mischance happened — we were lodging at the Red Lion where I woke in the dark to find my arm dead under my new husband's weight — the dead arm a terrifying object which I pulled free — but I could do nothing with it nor feel anything nor stop the thing flopping as an awful helpless weight on my chest — yet although I was silently sobbing with panic I dared not wake him (isn't this the rummest thing of all?) until by chafing kneading smacking I induced the first stab and tingle of blood to reach beyond the elbow and down into my forearm where the flesh felt wafered like leaves wrapped around bone and until finally the first cold filaments of pain crept into my fingers — only then did I bring myself to shake his shoulder to wake him and let out the sobs I had been containing "You only dreamt it" he said —

So much for Chipping Sodbury —

The following morning we fled to Bristol (at the time I thought we flew but we fled) and those among our ladies who could truly be called disciples met us there — Mr Moloch soothed my outrage against any who chose not to come by promising that we should find infinite reserves of genteel English people on the way over — at sixteen I was not inclined to argue on an issue which went far beyond whether a mouse (or an Indian) could be said to be God's own — and he assured me the prospective disciples would include "ladies who will not tolerate Baal or the Jesuits!"

You know he never was able to fly for me a second time — though he did try now and again if the ambition took hold of him — which is why his miracle with Louisa became such a turning-point and why he could not forgive me — but to be fair he has a heart even if he is not very clever so he never used our unhappiness to denounce me — the things that went wrong between us were never the subject of confessions — I have to say this for him.

Where was I with my story?

As I've explained — I can call every detail to mind — fresh as it was when I lived it for the first time — in fact it dogs me and won't leave me in peace — the terror of being lost — and myself as a pregnant young woman seeming quite separate from me as the observing intelligence — she in a panic and I calm — panting in the heat she is out of the gully at last! and being helped again by the native creatures who have returned to support her because they seem to know everything and welcome her again though some appear afraid to reach out or touch or offer her food while they chatter among themselves shyly covering their faces — she sees kind eyes as well as fearful eyes — indeed more kindness than any stranger has shown for a long time so she joins the laughter when they laugh — later she walks with them into the bush among the inevitable horse skeletons of progress and the panic among small furry animals — feeling confident of their companionship until cunning night begins seeping out of crannies — hollows deep in moss are already full cups of night — night lifts each scale of bark on the trees and cradles each petal with its tender darkness which stains the very air she must take into her body if she is to live — filled with dark air she suffers neither hunger nor thirst — she gives back the darkness to the night sky as a single word of discovery "Women!" — realizing too late that this one foreign sound might be enough to frighten them away forever.

You can try doing without breath if you like and then you'll know how I felt.

She was a fool to believe she could seek a new place in life without giving up the situation she already had among her kind — a fool to believe she could deny such luxuries as the leisure for watching clouds pass or the leisure for savouring cups of tea — a fool for believing that however far one travels one can remain the same — a fool for thinking the reason why Mr Moloch had not argued against her and insisted on establishing his haven for the reborn Christ in England was that he knew what he was doing —

There among the rocks in the closing gloom she has spoken too soon and undone what she did and once again lost those whom she depended on —

She talks to herself where she has fallen on her back —
she lies in great discomfort while the last dim shreds of
light tear free from the high branches and she hears what
ravenous interest her presence is creating among the
swarms of insects that whine around her —

She asks a whole lot of questions out loud such as had
Flora deceived her all this time? had dear Ann felt an
anguish of her own when first learning that the nightshirts
were to be burnt and accepting the commission to replace
them? had Lady Edwina with her locked hip and her
assurances that she believed the coming child to be God's
own Son deceived her for some deeper cause than loyalty? —

"So what we have instead of life" she says aloud to
herself in the language which did not belong to that place
"is mere poetry" —

Do you see that both pictures have come together Sergeant Arrell? the sad little waif who stumbled out of the
Gloucestershire woods has become the sad little waif
spreadeagled on foreign soil? and that she finds she feels
more defiantly alive the closer the risk of death approaches
in this childlike world crammed with moonlit posies of
leaves on giant stems (would the forest seem so big if she
were not so small?) yet she likes it here and she refuses
to go on trying so hard to understand her husband because
the effort diminishes her and magnifies him.

Enough of the husband —

As for her father — forget about that mouse! just remember him striking her terribly hard even when they

were already out in the street which made matters worse — his glove did not cushion the bright edges of pain and she smelled a swish of leather in the air —

So she has fallen — she is alone — she dreams of walking home to Mrs Boulton's mission and revenging herself by smashing down the Hidden Stars' routines for the terrible world to flood in and do its work — yet an insurrection of contentment already seeps along her limbs — the baby kicks — setting a sweetness sweeter than honeysuckle whispering through the newly darkening and shadowy night (has she drifted into sleep or is this an hallucination?) the dream wants her to eat and drink and to tie her laces again because now she is no longer the child who failed to learn how — also to struggle up on her feet and for this purpose the dream shakes its grizzled beard at her and bows its trembling neglect of hair while listening at her chest to hear if her heart still beats and then listening separately for the baby's heart —

The women went a while ago — she is alone with the dream —

Although he smells like a wood moth he remembers his manners and only gingerly touches her face with an enquiry and his fingers test only one sample of her hair which he appears to find unsatisfactory — does he know that her mother's hair is more beautiful? — her own courage astonishes her when she finds her voice which was lost on the word "women" and calmly explains to the dream that he is merely a dream though she must thank him for being a dream at all — while his eye buds a single tear too gummy to fall and too fluid to be withdrawn.

Well do you see her as she struggles up at last and accepts his hand? she finds the going easier for his help so she is grateful and she wants to share with him the text from Mr Moloch's last sermon "A life for a life — an eye for an eye — a tooth for a tooth — a foot for a foot — a hand for a hand — a wound for a wound — a bruise for a bruise!" she stops in horror —

The dream stops beside her but lets go of her hand while the childlike forest blooms moonshine and night birds sing around her head inside which she is thinking that a life for a life was precisely what Mr Moloch had had of her — as well as adding together Lavinia's missing breast and Charlotte's missing eye besides her own missing toe and so forth —

With this she pushes the dream away and faces him in the full shock of coming to her senses — she recognizes him as a figure common to all those fables about men of her own race shipwrecked and marooned and so robbed of respectability that they are left with not even a rag to their name —

All the more contrary of her then that when the dream reaches out to take her hand again she allows him to do so and she actually permits some alchemy to flow between them so that their grief mingles — just as well she is not herself today! — the dream repeats the very fault in Muley Moloch she now most bitterly resents by holding on to her as if the only knowledge he has is the knowledge he has through her — he lifts a thorny vine from her path as *their* vine.

It is no use trying to hurry me into using the simple brutal words you are after — because then there is no chance of explaining the facts of the matter so that you will understand what I tell you.

A familiar resentment hints that this could be her husband's wild spirit on the loose — her husband's spirit in exile among grim black trunks where wheeling bats utter shrill screams against the approaching dawn — then her attention is arrested by a spark of light — she glimpses it ahead — sees it move — she looks to her companion for an explanation and discovers he does not know how to meet her eyes —

Up ahead the light wanders on — winks and winks out —

She is staggering under her inherited ignorance so that she cannot even say whether she is glad or terrified at the prospect of rescue — or if rescue was what she wanted or precisely what she did not want when the light winks again and creeps jerkily to the left —

Her dream mumbles a name — Mrs Somebody — but it is not her name and he stands back while she stumbles ahead — awake and unaided — she spares only a moment of the dawning light to look him over — to look at his hollow face at his battered hands at his scabbed feet while her heart jumps so painfully that the child is shocked into utter stillness — which frightens her with how far she is from safety and how much she has fallen victim to the madness of neither staying in the security of Stroud nor domesticating her prophet at the mission —

Those filthy naked feet are enough to make her shudder — and yet curiously she knows her dream person is good — in this world nothing can be in between except Purgatory itself — everything is either good or evil —

Ahead the feeble spark of light leads on into the pallid morning and this time she notices half a dozen more lanterns (all at a distance) converging around it — some of them breaking into several points — the bat population spirals above her to make the air crackle like invisible paper and she can feel the forest's greenness on her skin — yet even while she strains to make out what the lights might signify they fade and turn pinkish with fatigue — those which had moved falter to a standstill and the one remaining in the same place goes out completely — in alarm she stumbles their way and then they flutter on a dying breath when the new sky floods down around everything to douse them altogether and rob her of guidance and swamp her in brilliant loss —

She has been wandering the whole night —

Two laughing jackasses on the same branch tilt their beaks toward Heaven to let out ripples of gleeful cackling to wake the entire forest as sun rays begin slanting among the trees and a breeze thin as a finger draws cold tear-tracks down her cheeks — she puts her hands to her hair which has come loose and pins it up — the sleeves fall back to her elbows and a delicious morning caresses the tender inner side of her bare arms —

Time and again she refuses to panic because God *has* to look after the baby so she tells the baby that as long as they keep facing into the sun they must be heading east and at worst they will reach the coastal road by midday —

You see she did come to herself —

She woke from the nightmare of goodness in sordid guise — and stepped right into a situation promising immediate help because there in a culvert stood a warm horse all by itself munching some grass and paying no heed to the log it was tethered to — the fact of the rider being nowhere to be seen was neither here nor there — the animal appeared fresh and possibly its saddlebags were still full so she went up to it and spoke and rubbed its nose — this was a placid horse quite unconcerned about strangers and determined not to miss a mouthful — but whose horse was it? she heaved herself up the embankment to look out for somebody — only to find she was in the presence of evil —

A little black tent was what caught her eye — as well as three wooden legs and two human legs supporting it — renewing the unwanted pain of a scene at Cuttajo cliffs — black velvet cloth — as she now saw — with satin piping

which struck her as grand enough to be a Spanish cape
or a shroud for some highborn ogre with waxy eyelids
and a lace collar —

She shook all over at the risk she was about to take —
yet she took it — though I don't recall her saying anything more than a timid "Excuse me" can you believe!

I beg your pardon for laughing (when will I be free of
this frightful cough?) but if you could have seen how the
fellow jumped! well the tent practically fell over sideways
while a nice young individual struggled out blushing with
guilt — I was conscious of my aloneness and the singu-
larity of our cause as the Household of Hidden Stars —
I felt proud —

"You need not worry" I assured him "I know what this
contraption is" — the morning was mounting higher so
that but for the forest shade the sun might already have
been uncomfortably hot — "yours is not the first camera
to be seen" — though why was he so abashed? —

He introduced himself as Charles Bailey — none
other — but in those days I had never heard of Charles
Bailey — cold clear blue eyes searched me with a deliciously dangerous look — then we shook hands which
was how I became aware that I had left my gloves at the
mission because I recoiled from contact with his skin —
not that he wasn't a pleasing person but my mind jolted
me back into the dream and the horny feel of another
man's hand — it made me nearly faint I can tell you —
so I was grateful of the diversion when he asked if I had

actually looked through any of the previous cameras I had seen — and nervously lifted the hem of the tent for me —

During the first few moments the misty glass square presented a puzzle until I discovered it could be managed and that the image was entrancing because one had to create it from a jumbled pattern of light — a mere shimmer of colour you see — the glass lost its pearliness and I found myself looking straight into a living picture — a picture more like a jewel than a painting — of an upside-down place in miniature —

But how was it there in all that undergrowth?

I had noticed nothing ahead of the photographer except a dense thicket yet here I was peeping through the leaves to discover a different world — I remained under the black cloth while with appalling clarity each detail displayed for me impressed itself topsy-turvy on my mind — particle by particle — goose pimples crawled about my arms as I made sense of the scene.

I understand perfectly! you are asking about Mr Moloch but I am telling you this is not the point! because you don't even know who he is — or whether indeed he did have another accident at sea perhaps!

You are too late to save anybody so why should you be in a hurry? — if it is a question of protecting the people at risk I would point out that Miss Theuerkauf and I are defenceless ladies who perpetually live in fear of being robbed or assaulted in our beds at night — and have done so ever since Mr Moloch first left us eighteen years ago — even though in other respects we managed quite nicely without a man on the place — mainly thanks to Louisa ("You'll be trying to learn how is this?" as she says "Well this is *so*!").

Lady Edwina? Edwina passed away only last April.

You were Edwina's favourite of all our neighbours' children — I've no doubt you remember how she spoiled you when you came over from your papa's place to muck out the stables for us though your sister refused violin lessons from Charlotte for fear of what the priest would say — apparently that Father O'Shaughnessy of yours made a habit of denouncing us as lost souls — wasn't this the truth? — and we called you Tiger.

I must say it is very vexing to have Master Bailey of all people dredge up that old incident which in my opinion scarcely reflected credit on him! I have never believed he went there to photograph a miracle at all (speaking personally — as the witness who saw the prophet's shoes rise off the carpet — one has no need of a postcard to remember a miracle by!) so much for photography —

And did any of us forget how Mr Moloch raised the dead? — of course not! — even when Charlotte lost her faith and invited him to admit that Louisa's heart might never have stopped our memories were too powerfully against her so we dismissed the argument that breathing can become shallow enough to escape detection — and Charlotte got the reputation of a backslider — her doubts merely united us against her and incidentally went a good way to improving Louisa's popularity —

Louisa saw a golden light and felt free of the flesh even to being able to watch her own body tossed senseless among the waves followed by the horror of reluctantly answering Mr Moloch's call so that she resisted his power and endured agonies while he drew her back from the brink of Paradise —

But these are not things one may subject to proof without undermining the beauty of faith — surely Bailey has the intelligence to see that the very presence of his camera would have been enough to prevent a chance miracle happening at that particular moment in any case? — and just look at the effect it might have had on poor Mr Moloch who was born with a gift he could never live up to —

It's so callous —

Perhaps both men were the worse for not going to war — people do not realize what it is for a man to have no war to go to in his lifetime — I hope your generation will be more lucky —

Mr Moloch's problem is that he is not the type to impress other males which I dare say is why he was driven to surround himself with women and I certainly do not wish you to think I sit in judgement of his vulgarity when quite the contrary I am fascinated by it — in a funny sort of way I admire it — as part of his inspiration and his gift of preaching with authentic fire —

What can a mere photographer know? —

I recollect so many many sermons it is hopeless to try conveying how they enriched us — me especially — especially at times when I was brought so low by punishments I succumbed to the creeping fear that I was being turned into nothing more than a slave — some of the sermons were based on stories I told *him* from my memories of Miss Honeywood's Sunday school — like the triumph of Saint Thomas over King Gundafar.

You've never heard of King Gundafar? but you must know how Doubting Thomas at the Last Supper thrust his hand in Christ's wounded side and all that? yes well this same apostle Thomas went to India to spread the word you see and arrived at the court of King Gundafar where he was warmly received — not because the king was persuaded about Jesus Christ as saviour of the world I'm afraid but because Thomas like Jesus was a carpenter (did you know the name Thomas means "twin"?) and by all accounts an exceptionally talented carpenter too or at least the Hindoos thought so — their King Gundafar who was much loved owing to his habit of believing what he was told (coupled with his other habit of spending rather too freely) promptly invited the apostle to build him a new palace and supported the offer with a large sum of money —

Now although Gundafar was loved by his people these people lived in such terrible poverty that Saint Thomas pledged himself to do something about it and spent the money on building shelters for them — money the king had paid for a palace — he housed and fed the sick and tended them — not to mention giving away handsome amounts to beggars and the like —

Well even the carefree Gundafar was bound to hear of it sooner or later so he called for Thomas to report on his progress with the palace and of course Thomas would never tell a lie which meant he was thrown in jail — so the apostle who had always expected the worst got what he expected —

For many years he lived as a convict in chains until the time came when the king's brother died and the whole country went into mourning because this prince had lived a pure life which of course meant he would go straight to Heaven — when he got there they showed him many marvels but none more dazzling among all the dazzling sights of Heaven than one particular unfinished palace so he asked "Who is to live here for all eternity?" and was told "This is the palace being built for King Gundafar by the apostle Thomas" —

As you may imagine the prince begged the Almighty to allow him to return to Earth for just long enough to whisper a message in his brother's ear — which is how Saint Thomas came to be let out of prison and King Gundafar with all his people was converted to the true faith — no doubt leading to a positive festival of mutual congratulations —

So pause before judging our humble home —

And before judging Muley Moloch for that matter —
though no one sees much of him in town these days apart
from his annual trip to buy grain and seed-potatoes besides
his visits to the coast to fit the giants of "Paradise" with
shoes half a dozen sizes larger than the largest available
in any shop — and the day he comes home he unfailingly
raises his cap to me like a family servant and calls over
the fence "Good morning Miss Byrne" with eyes going
grey as mist — so I feel my heart turn and remember
when we first invited him back to live at the mission —
he cried out in a loud voice "Surely you cannot forgive
me! and nor can she! and nor can I forgive myself!" —

What I might need to forgive him *for* is between the
two of us and shall remain so — but what Louisa could
possibly need to forgive is a mystery — though I suppose
one ought not to forget the sight I saw in that upside-
down square of light shown me by Charles Bailey's
photographic camera.

Didn't I say?

Each detail had been carved with a scalpel and set in
poisoned silence — showing the Stars in miniature —
some with their backs to me and some facing me — each
well-known back unmistakable and each face of those
looking my way offering the dwindled version of a familiar
expression — while between them lay a trench into which
they gazed — where I saw a dishevelled Louisa perspiring
and bent over — miraculously upside down you must
remember — settling to a man's task — dumping a

shovel load of clay on the rim of the trench — she was
doing Muley Moloch's work for him —

The instant I saw her I found I could also hear her
panting breath — plus the scrape of metal against
stone — for the first time I was struck by the fact that
she had survived untouched by the consumption afflicting
most of the rest of us in one degree or another —

I could also hear the photographer right near me fret-
ting impatiently — not daring to remove the tent and
take back his camera he began knocking one boot heel
against the other and letting out exasperated sighs —
much I cared! — I was hypnotized at my peephole because now I had the picture clear I still could not make
out what it might mean — then I saw something which
had previously eluded me — a body laid to one side —
and the frightful inverted slackness of it —

I must have flinched because I lost the picture for a
few seconds — unable to find the correct angle to assemble it again — hearing young Bailey remove the screw
caps from his chemical bottles — liquids gurgled —
odours cut my breath — I could delay no longer — I
knew now what he was up to —

Incensed at his indecent prying I threw off the cloth —
only to find myself blinded by a shimmering mass of
daylight — I believe I wavered and stumbled and fell
against him even as he painted his Satanic mixture on a
photographic plate ready to slide it into the machine —

I knew by report how the device worked — that an

image would begin to be magically printed there — each
detail of Louisa's bare arms and perspiring immodesty
etched forever in silver — also the unexplained body —
he had already snatched his black cloth and disappeared
under it when I barged forward through the thicket
screaming "Beware beware!" and suddenly found myself
grasped by Mr Moloch who stared wild-eyed at me and
restrained me as if I had lost my wits —

I screamed into his face "Beware of — beware of — !"
I choked — helpless as Lavinia — the necessary word
would not come — while ladies stood round the graveside
stupid with alarm like statuary in a teaching studio (this
one representing Horror and that one Grief) — but already Mr Moloch had begun shouting on his own account — shouting at me about the baby while I struggled
against him —

I felt my own sobs yet I could find no voice for making
sense of what I knew — until Ann having put her head
near mine and heard me whisper that we were being pried
upon led them in among the leaves (Charlotte and Hester
and Martha and the exhausted Louisa) while it was I who
now clung to Mr Moloch because I found myself staring
down into Flora's dead face and the sight struck me dumb
with guilt that perhaps this death *had* been my doing —

Once his anger swept through him — as when the
demons were routed — my husband broke free from my
encumbrance and bounded in among the trampled
branches where the black tent had already been flung aside

and the offender — though dragged to his knees by ladies — still held the precious photographic plate in one hand to keep it safe from harm —

Mr Moloch's problem was that he didn't know which way to turn —

His suspicious manner of squinting at the camera showed how little he understood — this brought me to my feet in a flash I can tell you because I realized that an empty camera was harmless — but already in those lost moments young Bailey acted swiftly and slipped free — he charged off through the bracken still with the clean plate in his hand and the belated prophet in pursuit —

Bailey paused — he turned and struck Mr Moloch a terrible blow full in the face — sent the poor prophet stumbling about in shock and pain with a broken nose gushing blood — then doubled back to hoist his camera complete with frail legs in the crook of his elbow — and leapt down the slope to where his horse nibbled the grass —

Because the Stars had their skirts and their modesty to contend with it looked as if the miscreant might get away — taking his stolen scene of ladies sweating at a grave for a body dead of no visible cause — when a queer spindly figure stepped out from among the trees — a ginger-bearded oddity — bones bundled together and netted in ugly veins —

Well the horse shied and no wonder! —

Mr Bailey dropped the plate while he clutched the reins

and tried to protect his precious camera — this gave me my chance to dart in — but do you think I could get hold of the beastly thing? not a bit of it! — the slippery stuff made me drop it so all I could do (holding my swollen body) was stamp and grind it under my heel —

When I looked up from this work the figure out of my dream was gone (yes I recognized him and my stomach turned) Mr Moloch caught hold of the photographer's ankle to dislodge him from the saddle only to be knocked over for the second time — then the photographer hitched the heavy camera on his shoulder — swung up into the saddle again — and rode away at a trot like a species of equestrian cripple — not fully in his seat and unable to right himself —

The shame of it! the trespass! the breach of privacy!

I went to Mr Moloch's assistance — only then did I enjoy relief at having found my way home.

When my husband left the mission for good and went to live in Bunda — and you might consider this perverse — he rented a shop next door to Mr Bailey's photographic studio — between Bailey and Brewster's Mercery Emporium —

But who has ever fathomed the human heart or its fears? —

Take for instance Lavinia's shrill insistence that we report the intrusion to whatever authorities might be in the area (a passion we only understood when she had been sufficiently whipped to confess her lascivious desires with catalogues of desperate wrong words — poor thing) — one felt habitually sorry for Lavinia because a single glance from those uncertain eyes was enough to give warning that even at her best her politeness might be no more than vacancy.

Before assuming the name Muley Moloch my husband was known to style himself Prince of the Hebrews —

To this day he still dreams of leading us to the Holy Land (being a thorough come-outer always did suit him) — yes he is back with us and indeed he very well might lead us there for all I know — though he declines to predict when — maybe from self-consciousness about his lack of education in arithmetic —

Hopeless as he has always been in the arithmetical department the one number Muley Moloch enshrined in every sermon with complete certainty was the thousand-year kingdom of the returned Christ — to begin with the Second Coming and to last until the Day of Judgement —

As I have said before — inspiration has nothing to do

with how educated a person is — and who can say where the Holy Land is any longer? —

If you are surprised at his choice of companions in this great purpose allow me to point out that from the moment his family apprenticed him to the trade of bootmaker — on account of being lame like his father — he was thrown in among dwarfs and cripples so perhaps this was what gave him strength to cope with us — though I won't be questioned any more about the missing bits — like my toe — because in the long run that doesn't matter to me —

You say you want facts — well if you are to understand what the facts mean you must hear me out — we suffered what we suffered in order to fit ourselves for the Second Coming — Jesus being in our minds every hour of the day — and hymns on our lips keeping us in a state of ecstasy so we would not be caught napping.

Please make yourself comfortable.

Since you left me last night I have not moved from this chair — but don't mention nightmares!

You must have noticed how one's daytime shadow is only normal body size (see my hand there on the floor?) while at night by lamplight it grows monstrous? — well the past is like that too and even the sober truth seems not much more comfortable than the truth of the tannery —

Come to think of it the tannery is what most people

know about — certainly the convicts did — and we de-
ceive ourselves if we think our world of little luxuries and
neat lawns does not need to be paid for or that it is we
who do the paying — I include your grandfather who
paid by going away to fight for Queen Victoria in the
Indian Mutiny — forgive me but how wonderfully it
would shock my dear parents to hear me sounding like
the odious Mr Owen who Judge Honeywood's daughter
always said deserved the gallows —

My life used to be a prison of obedience though I've
no patience at all with that kind of thing now —

Have you thought how few pleasures the polite woman
enjoys while confined to the drawing-room at her em-
broidery frame or at the pianoforte or simpering after
eligible brutes who look her over with an eye for cattle
before riding off to meet one another later (and with equal
gratification) at a boxing ring where they pay to watch
men's faces being pummelled until they bleed? —

A nice prospect!

The polite woman whether she's in Cheltenham or Melbourne — writes letters and does wool work — she dips
into Thackeray perhaps and writes more letters — she
arranges dried flowers and perhaps walks in her garden
before settling down to write more letters — why does
she write so many letters? because the letters go out into
the world and travel where she would wish to be free to
travel in person — they speak to people while she — in
the loneliness of good manners — merely tittletattles

with neighbours of an acceptable kind about matters from which good manners preclude any subject that might touch her heart —

But the sufferers are not necessarily anxious to change things — not at all! — they accommodate themselves to being deceived — here at the mission we faced the truth — we transcended letters having really travelled — and to the remotest place possible — we despised substitutes so we never rebelled against our squalid punishments — or our duties — even when Mr Moloch put a ban on stylish clothes and we had to wear woollen dresses intended to look ugly did we complain? — indeed I distinctly remember the first time I went to town wearing my brown horror I stepped down out of the sulky free from the squirmings I had felt at home — filled with gaiety and pride!

From a bird's-eye view the mission farm began as a cluster of four roofs almost wholly enveloped in undergrowth — three buildings enclosing a yard and the stables halfway along a track to our creek where the patch cleared for a garden was already matted with weeds — here the returning Christ would find us —

Very different from the place as it is today —

Into this neglect our party of pioneers arrived (with one about to die and one still not fully brought back to life) to hack at the choking plants and lay bare a ring of land around each hut — after the convicts left it was we women who wielded the mattocks to chip out the scrub — even in rain women wearing waterproof cloaks with hoods and carrying rakes rustled down to the garden — right through the winter months the clearing work went on — heaps of weeds being burned on dry days — and Mr Moloch in his shirtsleeves darting about doing twice as much as anybody while he taught us the practical use of tools — then in spring when the picket fences had been repaired and new ones built for protecting the lawn and garden against intruding wallabies (who learnt to become famous connoisseurs of lettuce and peach-tree leaves) we sowed the seeds purchased from Melbourne and planted dozens of cuttings sold us by various neighbours at Yandilli —

This was to be our living you see — the produce of our market garden was to pay for meat flour butter and tea despite the fact that most of us had never so much as grown a tray of mustard seed! — to our surprise Lady Edwina confessed herself quite an expert — right till her dying day she swore that even if the faith had not sustained her and the nearness of Jesus in those days she would not have missed creating our garden for worlds —

So you must imagine lots of seedlings sprouting in rows and fruit trees putting out blossom while Martha Sparrow (our only source of medical knowledge) gasped and choked to death — and you must imagine the crops being picked for delivery twice a week to Yandilli in the spring cart with Hester taking the reins and Ann for company — then so much fruit ripening at Christmas that we could scarcely keep pace with bedding our precious apricots and peaches in boxes or filling buckets with plums while Elizabeth Eyre brought sandwiches from the kitchen and Mr Moloch worked a hand-pump to fill the tank from the creek — you must imagine such a joyous harvest that when we dragged our bone-weary bodies indoors at dusk — drawn home by the aromas of Elizabeth's cooking — we sang marching hymns to the rhythmic clash of tools and the whir of Mr Moloch's lawn mower as he used the last minutes of light to indulge his pet hobby of taming the native grass —

The only other time we sought help — as I have explained — was with building our chapel which took seventy-seven slabs of squared bark for the walls and twenty-three for roofing and roof caps — all clamped on to the frame and with a second frame clamped on outside to hold them flat — you may count them for yourself if you wish and see how wonderfully they have lasted —

Mind you we look after the place.

We were a closed community so there was no one but us — no teaching program for novices no converts no hospital no food-kitchen no refuge for fallen women and not much contact with the town besides the stories Ann brought back after marketing our produce (until her whiskers grew and she passed the job entirely to Hester) — a closed community with bush all round us spreading for hundreds of miles inland like a thick blanket on the ridges and choking the gullies between —

This vast tangle of vegetation assailed us with leafy smells foreign to our garden so we felt the constant seductive lure of adventure — and sometimes of a morning when walking in the forest we would come upon two men or perhaps a man and a lad seated on the ground sipping hot tea from pannikins while their campfire smouldered and the fern-trees rustled against a simple canvas tent held up by two forked stakes with a pole between — smoke always hung deliciously among the leaves — generally the man would scramble to his feet politely enough but the lad most often just pushed his cap back off his forehead and stretched his legs to show off their length in long leather gaiters reaching right up to the knee — sometimes the man would offer us hospitality and point to a billy hung over the embers on a miniature version of the tent frame but we always hurried off regretfully because the scene filled us with intolerable yearnings for the sweetness of lounging like that all night by a fire with nothing to do but watch it blaze and die down and break to ash while the encircling night widened into the clear dark and treetops spangled with brilliant stars filled the sky —

Not to mention the tales we heard of explorers finding passes through the mountains beyond which they discovered grasslands as far as the eye could see and eventually reached a desert which they promptly set out to cross by foot — earning a name for amazing courage when all they were suffering as men was what we women longed to be at liberty to attempt for the sheer pleasure of its limitless freedom —

Instead we bound ourselves to our routines and wasted our eloquence on the apples and cabbages we took to town for selling to people who stared at us and gossiped behind their hands to humiliate us — but what they did not know was that this gave us courage because we saw we were as far beyond their bondage to drudgery as the explorers were beyond ours —

Anyway who is to say precisely what humiliation is? —

Take the case of Mr Moloch where the photographer Charles Bailey was concerned — years and years before they occupied neighbouring shops — what can account for the prophet's visit to the studio (only nine weeks after the rout I described to you last night) to lay before him the most curious request the young scamp was ever likely to hear? —

What business had Mr Moloch as a man of God with such a shocker? and yet I have a suspicion my husband felt able to put the proposition because he knew he *was* putting it to a shocker — and that a more conventional man would call the police without further ado — no offence intended — so Bailey it had to be —

And when he recovered from being struck speechless he consented to think the matter over —

Meanwhile Flora had been months in her grave and I

was confined to bed with the impending birth of my famous child — the expectation gripping our Household grew too intense to be described so let me simply point out the fact that everyone forgot about spying on everyone else and even Hester was touched for once with maidenly kindness —

Towards me they were angels — absolute angels!

Being confined to bed again gave me such a lot of time and energy for thinking I became obsessed by the *unfairness* of fate when I thought of poor dear Beatrice still back there in the hot stony ground on Ascension Island while I luxuriated between the sheets awaiting the arrival of a baby who would be the saviour of us all — not only had poor Beatrice lived her entire life without ever knowing the flustered elation of placing one's hands on one's tummy to feel movements under the skin but now neither she nor Elizabeth Eyre nor Flora would share in the fearful prospect of helping guide the child as he grew (for it was certain he must be a boy) to face the task of wrestling against a world gone mad on the wickedness of electrical things and steam engines — not to mention photographs I suppose! — and expecting to satisfy its greed like a rabble of Digby Barnetts picking up nuggets of gold without even the need of honest labour — a world the poorer for losing these dear ladies —

Even more surprising was the idea that fate had also been unfair to Louisa Theuerkauf — her unrequited love for my husband might well have given her reason for turning into a complainer yet she refused to complain —

Well a full week before the baby was due everything at the mission stood spotless and in perfect readiness while friends sat with me all through the day and night to await the first sign and young Charles Bailey rode up on his horse to ask if he might camp down by the stream — in case you are wondering I have to explain that I did feel terribly agitated by this arrangement and could only calm my fears with the thought that nothing mattered compared to the fact of the miracle happening in my body —

Naturally I knew how supremely significant the occasion was and that I must make sacrifices — but to have myself photographed! — to have the very moment of birth photographed! — well it violated every instinct —

Privacy a thing of the past —

I was to become the most public figure in history since the Virgin Mary and even my happiness could not be thought of as private because it must be shared by all true believers throughout the world —

Charles Bailey being so tall and strongly made was really quite handsome and a frock coat looked very well on him if you could see past his oddities (no I haven't set eyes on him for years) because in those days he had a long thick neck supporting a rather insignificant head but his *manner* left everything to be desired in that he ducked and leered — a real specimen of a primitive! — and set his big hands hovering around the equipment — even around the subject which in this case was me in my bed if you please!

I thought I should never endure the shame but I was no longer a private person and had little choice so his camera on its props faced me for many days until the glass eye began to seem scarcely more intrusive than the mirror in the corner or our own table with a bowl of water upon it —

Now and again Mr Bailey would amble in bringing his black cloth and request permission to check whether all was still in readiness — on one occasion he asked for my bed to be pushed right against the windowsill to make maximum use of the light "What if the baby comes after dark?" the evil Hester Partington asked and we all laughed but Mr Moloch dismissed the possibility because why else had God inspired some inventor to construct a camera if it not for the sake of this occasion? — he was right —

I believe Charles Bailey began to think of himself as one of the Chosen —

The camera peered straight at me from the end of the bed exactly between my feet — generally simply the eye of a box but from time to time (as happened on the morning of my worst pains) the eye of a humped black-shrouded human shape filling me with unspeakable horror particularly when the midwives — which is to say Elizabeth Canning who knew what to do but was hampered by her wheelchair and Louisa who did not know what to do — stripped back the bedding and strapped my legs in position while Hester sounded the alert which brought Hidden Stars from all quarters still fresh with the odours of interrupted duties — I caught a whiff of smoke from the boiler fire and a warm horse smell from the stables — then I was suddenly beyond noticing anything and thank Heaven the physical pain was too savage for me to care about the camera or the anguish suffered by my modesty at the first nauseating exposure.

So now perhaps you begin to suspect what class of witness you were listening to when you let Master Bailey have his say!

How many photographs he took I do not know but he left when the ladies covered me with sheets — my only memory of his departure is a brief tableau of him picking up his packed equipment and shaking my husband's hand — he said nothing to me and avoided acknowledging me at all — as he went he nodded generally to the Stars who stood back from my bed shakily singing hymns while Louisa at the washbasin turned my way too with her hands dripping soapy water and released that glorious voice to soar high above theirs in a free descant —

My baby boy was perfect —

Then and there we christened him Immanuel while the prophet Moloch recited Isaiah's famous words "Behold a virgin shall conceive and bear a son and shall call his name Immanuel *God with us*" — you might have expected hovering angels to join in the refrain — you might at least have expected me to be filled with unspeakable joy at having found favour with God — quite the contrary — the whole event struck me as somehow rehearsed to death (do you know that?) besides being irrelevant to the precious little bundle warm in my arms — so it is no good complaining that God does not send us presentiments —

Hester asked "Are you sure Baby isn't a dwarf?"

I felt more like a mother with the ordinary exhaustion of having delivered a new life than the Mother of God despite all the tiptoeing and the hallelujahs going on around me — not to mention old friends being too shy even to meet my eyes — the truth is that I felt overwhelmed by fear because my baby would surely be found out and exposed as nothing more extraordinary than a human child of the usual kind — yet at the same time what could be better? and this was precisely what I wished to prove so I could forget every other duty apart from relishing the simple joy of a mother — accordingly I stirred my memory again in desperation for some hint of how my pregnancy might have happened except through God — inventing wild tales of forgotten moments and farfetched transmissions — wary in case somebody might read these thoughts and report me as a heretic — let me tell you this hidden palpitation was worse than anything — meanwhile my baby began to squirm under my nightdress and to feed from my breast so that the pain of surprise came as the deepest pleasure I had ever known — filling me with pity for Lavinia especially —

Lavinia — you'll remember — had only one breast because the left side failed to grow when she was a girl — she wouldn't even have been any use as an Amazon unless she learned to fire a bow left-handed — peculiar people those Trojan women — and they say there were also other Amazons in Africa cutting off one breast — imagine the frightful great wound left there and how did the skin ever grow back? not to mention what a cut-off breast might look like by itself — let's say just forgotten on a table — still with the cut-off section of her tunic partly covering it — it makes me shiver even now — and I never felt quite at ease with Lavinia once I had marked her with this idea —

I began to feel so sorry for the legless Elizabeth (saying "Botheration!" while she managed wonderfully) that the tears streamed from my eyes — and sorry for Ann who grumbled "How should I know where a handkerchief is?" even while she produced one and passed it to me —

What more can I say? in any case — ssh! — here comes Louisa to offer us some luncheon.

There have been scenes of dreadful treachery here-abouts — you will certainly have heard how Mrs Atholl shot her husband in a most unnatural manner and was treated treacherously in her turn by your neighbour dear old Mr Earnshaw (still in good health I trust?) cases of secret revenge by convicts against former masters though I mention no names — and by violated girls against seducers —

Frightful things happen in this parish involving knives and poisonings not to mention the natives — such fright-

ful things that I am surprised you can find time to visit
me day after day simply for the sake of adding another
gory item to the catalogue — because what has been done
cannot be undone — and as for justice there are issues
more important than justice all things considered!

I beg your pardon? yes of course you knew Immanuel
with the two of you being near enough the same age —
you must remember how adorable he was as he grew up
and what a great favourite with the Household — his
sunny ways cleansed us of staleness just by filling the
mission with chatter — no one could doubt he was
already our saviour which made it all the more urgent to
decide how we should prepare him for the unthinkable
responsibility he had to face —

The answer in the Bible was that God Himself revealed
the truth to Jesus saying "Thou art my beloved son in
whom I am well pleased" — admittedly this might take
one problem off our hands — but before any such an-
nouncement could be made Jesus had to be raised in
hiding from the wrath of Herod and taught the carpenter's
craft by his father — well we decided to tell Immanuel
nothing so he could grow up healthy and useful as a
bootmaker's apprentice until the time came for him to be
called from On High —

We recorded the passing years on his baptismal robe
(because of course no one dared baptize him as a baby so
Ann cut the garment a suitable size for a growing lad) —
sitting round in the afternoon wearing our caps tied under

the chin with ribbons and our heads wagging as we talked each of us embroidered the white cotton with a flower for his birthday — ready for when he might be washed clean of original sin — for example Ann did a white rose and Elizabeth Canning did a white iris then there was a white carnation by Charlotte and Lavinia's white and gold honeysuckle woven in with my white lily while Lady Edwina — who used the excuse of shaky hands to cover the fact that she felt the task beneath her besides being too fiddly — read out loud to us and on one occasion was quite agog at coming across a mention of Captain Cook in a new book by Thackeray especially as Mr Thackeray claimed that a great number of the descriptive passages in *Cook's Voyages* were notoriously invented by Dr Hawkesworth who "did" the book — and we felt suitably superior since our experience was indubitably authentic — this was before Edwina shrivelled up because she turned out to be one of those women who do not so much age as desiccate.

No — Louisa never learned to embroider and she never apologized for her ignorance either.

My memory is clear today —

Of course in the sixth year Charlotte's carnations ceased when she died and the honeysuckle grew seriously crooked in the ninth year (I have to say I am reaching an age when I begin to doubt that either of those ladies caught the consumption from me yet undeniably we did spend a tremendous amount of time nursing sick people) —

My recovery became an example to all — others were punished for not living up to it —

Meanwhile Immanuel grew to be a terrible scamp who delighted in tricks and dreamed all through his lessons until we despaired of teaching him anything — though never big for his age he was too strong for us to hold — he tormented the goats and laughed when they chased him through the gate where they kicked holes all over Mr Moloch's lawn — poor Immanuel caught it that time — once he crossed from end to end of the apple orchard jumping from tree to tree through a ruin of blossoms — do you think we were delighted! — he teased the ladies in awful ways causing them to spill their tea and prick their fingers — except Ann who was his favourite — yet they forgave him and only the prophet had enough confidence to punish him as if he were an ordinary boy —

When he was ten he gave us a devastating fright by going missing — then at sunset returned home very tired but cheery to tell us his adventures down at a logging camp on the Yandilli road where he had talked to some axemen and watched a great tree fall — he spoke of that tree with awe — but no matter how we scolded him we made no progress against his wildness and he enjoyed a great deal of freedom because by this time he was trapping rabbits for the cook pot and could expect to be away from the house for hours at a stretch in any case —

Immanuel turned twelve (which was the age when Jesus

first preached in the temple) and yet God still did not intervene directly though we knew the boy needed to be told who he was — told soon — and shown that he had become our saviour already — loved by everyone for his freshness — that our lives had not always been so filled with joy — and that just as he had changed us without knowing so he must go forth and change the world —

If I had had a grain of sense I would have taken this on myself and spoken to him straight out in private — but did I do anything so simple or sensible? I did not —

My abiding weakness is that I have never been able to refuse anybody anything — well we devised a ceremony in which each of us could take some part — dressing him in that clean white gown and anointing his head and feet — except Louisa who would come into her own by singing "Rejoice rejoice rejoice greatly" you know the thing — well the communion table was set up on the lawn and a new lace cloth spread on it — dazzling under the sky — I think I can say we each felt God had never been nearer at hand while the boy himself simply shone until the moment when all the Stars instinctively stepped back at his approach —

He realized we were in earnest and I have never seen a face collapse as his face collapsed — I knew we were in the wrong and I thought of *you* — yes of you — because you once came down from the hills telling us you had seen some blood spots on a slab of stone and your father told you that this was what happened when the wild folk made a boy into a man — I thought does Tiger know a way of doing it at no more cost than a couple of drops of blood? —

"Aunt Ann" he cried and reached out to catch hold of her as she quickly slipped away to hide in the chapel (have you noticed the surprising dexterity of fat women?) "Mama" he called and I did find enough courage to clutch at his hand but in such a way I suppose that my humility hurt him all the more —

He bent down and grasped the hem of the robe to pull it up over his head — sweet lad — crumpling the flowers and struggling to free his arms from the sleeves and getting in such a state that by the time he tugged it off his face was bright as a strawberry — on the verge of tears he screwed up the lovely embroideries and trampled them underfoot in a passion of helplessness — then blundered away in pursuit of his favourite — letting the chapel door bang after him —

We followed and crowded into the blinding gloom — colliding with the boy who was already storming back to reach the prophet   "Papa" he demanded in the dark "tell me I am all right!" —

The air was so cool —

Well from that day Ann could never muster the spirit to be grumpy again even though she grew a beard which ought to have given her more cause than ever — and if you had been in a position to witness Mr Moloch's expression (as we were *not* in that dim place) I believe you might

have seen fear there when he replied "You are all right" —
certainly his voice took on so urgently serious a tone he
seemed to be indicating a deeper meaning — I can tell
you I have listened to him in my memory countless times
hoping to recapture that exact tone —

"Then why" Immanuel demanded "don't you smack
me for spoiling my shirt?" and he defied the prophet to
raise his hand — wanting it and aching for it and shrug-
ging off my protective embrace — so Mr Moloch came
close to peer at us — faceless silhouetted head turning
from the boy with his pleading eyes to me with mine —

"What am I to do?" he asked — and thus the beautiful
ceremony was ruined by questions —

Thin stripes of light scored our backs and shoulders
while every now and again a gleam caught the brilliant
tears in somebody's eye —

This was not how we had meant it to be — and from
that day forward the boy became absolutely uncontrol-
lable —

Cruel to our cats and neglectful of the pony he loved
he was more often running amok in the bush than
home — and when he did come in he would set about
washing his hands in the most compulsive way — no
sooner were they dry than he washed them again — and
then again — sometimes eight or nine repetitions until
I scolded him for wasting precious water — meanwhile
it was no better during dinner-time — he chewed the
food twenty times on one side of his mouth then chewed

it twenty times on the other before swallowing — a meal could last for hours let me tell you — ending in an infatuation with counting — counting the ticks of the clock and the calls of an owl in the pepper tree — the aggravation of it nearly drove us mad — he counted the number of steps he took to carry an empty bucket to the well and a full bucket back — till eventually he began a slow daydreaming sort of count which turned out to be the number of breaths he drew if you please!

Our joy had been shattered in the most unexpected way and no amount of prayer made the least impression — do you blame me if I felt horrified and tried to shock him out of this state by the most stinging remarks I could muster though I was never given to such boldness with anybody as a rule —

Quite soon another misfortune happened to him because his face lost its character — the brightness faded to a resentful expression — and when his mouth twisted he was suddenly shown as looking like no one so much as the prophet in the days when I first saw him deliver a sermon from a pulpit in Stroud — with prominent ears and a prominent nose — except that this smaller likeness refused to utter a word and indeed appeared to have lost the power of speech altogether —

The upshot was that we returned to our old solution — we blamed each other — although with one tremendous difference in that I no longer carried the brunt of the blame — a new reign of petty terrors started with beatings and humiliations and the penance of having to go without sleep — how deeply I knew it! but I could not resist the luxury of my new status — also I am ashamed to say I did enjoy the sin of revenge against those who like Hester had persecuted me through the years —

So as tension at the mission grew to an unbearable pitch Ann began coughing blood — I suppose we knew something must break —

One morning the sun's rays sloped among the tree trunks as usual — birds chattered and the busy life of the hateful bush took on its customary inane complexity while I stood in the yard — conscious of breathing free from pain (like the alien I was) — when the sky hollowed itself so that it drew all substance from everything — sucking the substance up into empty space — leaving the dry world discarded like an empty chrysalis — this was how it felt — "Immanuel!" I shrieked — already in panic and calling him again and again because somehow I knew he had gone —

Two of the sisters came running from the chapel — they let the door drift shut after them and stood blinking against the glare unconscious of the dusty stencilled knee marks on their skirts where they had knelt in prayer — or the scatter of cats — and suddenly the sky was full of clouds swooping down among the trees with shafts of sunlight lancing in under a turmoil of threatening vapours — you never saw anything so unexpected —

Oh I cannot bear to talk about it — you must forgive me Sergeant —

This cough is getting worse with summer.

You will judge me I am sure but when the Voice came back with its usual assurance I interpreted it as meaning that the lad had been taken to Heaven — our crisis was over — I felt ashamed of my doubts and relieved (yes) to be freed from the grand role thrust on me — "You may depend upon it that the Lord is coming!" was what I felt I was being told — so Immanuel *would* descend in a chariot of fire after all — and I sensed God closer than ever before —

At last I must have done something right!

Others of the Stars hurried in and out of doors conferring as they passed me — vanishing round the back of sheds to return a moment later with nothing but empty hands to show — Hester even peered down the well — and Mr Moloch emerged in his heavy boots unwrapping a gun so that I knew what he intended and found myself calling out "The boy is in his Father's keeping" —

All movement stopped while the faithful listened on every side — "Fear not!" I added while Mr Moloch shook all over as if to rid himself of some clinging pest and ordered them to look sharp —

"Bring whatever weapons you can find" he begged "while Hester rides to town for help" —

"Fear not" I cried out again and the Sisters glanced

from one to another bewildered "he is in his Father's hands!" I repeated because it seemed the right thing and smiles broke out —

"He has certainly gone" the crippled Elizabeth spoke up timidly to be sure I knew —

I replied "And the Lord be praised!" to which a number of them whispered "Amen" but my husband rewound the oilcloth around the breech of his weapon and strode towards me threateningly "Whatever the truth of the matter" he roared without respect "we cannot pretend to know — so we must do our duty the best we can" —

I simply smiled now I understood what power I had and explained "The Voice tells me" —

But he fumed in an even greater fury "What does the Voice tell you then?"

And I answered "That he is with his Father" —

There was a desperate light in Muley Moloch's face — which if I had ever seen previously I dare say I might have recognized for love — at least this is what I believe as I look back on it — seeing his whole body twist with the pain it cost him to defy me further "There is the danger of being lost in these wild woods — there is the danger of snakes — and there is the danger of demons" —

I smiled saying "Shouldn't we be mindful of Saint Luke's warning and be ready to forsake even our family if the Lord so wills it?" — he flinched because he had often quoted this to us as a text applying to our forbidden letters from home — I continued "Besides I have been

among the demons myself and found them simple people
whose whimsy it is to wish themselves back into the shapes
of animals" I had the authority of knowing my destiny
"but they laugh as we laugh" though in fact we seldom
did laugh —

"You dare put the boy at risk?" he raged —

I kept smiling and said "Can you not hear me? he has
gone to his Father's keeping" —

In the hush before the rain a whole flock of black
cockatoos dipped and flapped among the branches "I
am" he uttered these words more ferociously than any
curse "his father!"

You cannot imagine the solemn shock this produced
on the ladies who lacked my strength — yet God sent
no thunderbolt and when a few fat drops of rain thwacked
the soil and a few splashed against our faces Louisa seized
her moment "I have been the one who is raised from the
dead isn't it?" she took charge of the centre stage "to
me must even Mr Moloch tell the truth if Catherine is
wrong" —

My husband passed his wrapped-up gun from one useless hand to the other as he addressed the ground "I am
the father" he repeated —

Rain fell faster —

"Then how is your wife knowing nothing?" Louisa grew
to the stature of a judge —

"She did not know" he admitted vaguely (I invite you
to put yourself in my place at this moment Sergeant with

the earth opening under my feet and a void which I had seen briefly in the sky now happening inside me) "Catherine did not know" he repeated as if nothing more need be said —

I shrieked "*What* did I not know?"

All around us our voices could be heard to echo faintly in the empty mission buildings and faintly in the well — while I recognized anguish in my husband's face — a face disfigured by trickles of rain "She was too ill — " he explained and he looked up at me with pleading eyes " — to know" —

He was pleading for Immanuel — just as the love I glimpsed had not been for me but also for Immanuel.

I shall not say I was shaken with hatred because at that time I was too powerless to feel anything beyond my numb shell filled with loss — too blinded by the squalid shame of his confession to see anything beyond the dark spots appearing all over his clothes like a contagious disease.

I keep a diary and I spent last night reading through that very entry — eighteen years ago — you see I sometimes wonder whether Mr Moloch has any idea I loved him or how great a fool I made of myself leading us halfway round the world just to be able to live with him —

For his part I simply cannot tell if he hated me or if he was too self-conscious but he never had any sort of freedom with me despite the fact that he could share a joke with the others —

Little mouse that I was perhaps I did my destructive work at night in my dreams who knows? but the loss of my son drove me to such a state that Ann felt so disquieted on my behalf she grew preoccupied with my problems until one day on a ladder she missed her footing and broke her hip — next came poor little Lavinia whimpering as she hurried about her tasks and even though she always had been a bit cracked nothing prepared us for the stormy outbursts she suddenly let fly or her being found hiding in a cupboard when Hester drove back from town bringing a constable to have us investigated — I can never forgive Hester and at the time I could only marvel at the prophet's forbearance when he walked to the gate to let the policeman in and welcomed Hester with a ceremonial kiss on the cheek.

In Yandilli the cry had gone up that our entire mission should be burned down to cleanse it of contagion — and nothing less than the local lethargy could have saved us or our belongings — the others were ill and I was supposed to be possessed —

Yes the inquiry was carried out but it produced nothing definite despite the fact that my influence was now suspected everywhere from Adelaide to Brisbane — within a week of Oliver and Digby Barnett staking out a new farm down on the coast they were at each other's throats over the fate of their old selection and rumours that I had somehow bewitched them into leaving it — at least this is what Florence Love has told me since — and I have to admit that even at home Edwina became addicted to snuff

and left hideously stained handkerchiefs in the least expected places — and Mr Moloch took to shooting bullets
at a target for hours on end — not to mention reports
filtering in from Yandilli such as the news that a tin of
mutton was found to be blown after young Tommy
McNeil died of food poisoning (though one wondered
what a butcher's wife was doing feeding her family from
a tin!) even the Brian Boru Inn moved to Cuttajo to put
its customers at a safer distance from me and my grief —
the consequence of this was that your Father O'Shaughnessy found himself recalled in disgrace over a matter
connected with Mrs Gilbert the publican's wife and the
only spot of relief for the churchgoers was a surprisingly
cultured Welshman who arrived to take his place with
strict instructions (so we heard tell) to keep his hands off
the women of the parish —

At the heart of it all was the loss of Immanuel —

That superstitious nonsense was simply gossip — I am
a good Christian and a soldier of Christ — the grief which
had driven me to hate everything in sight came as a
cleansing fire because I was rebelling — eager for conflict
against all humankind so I couldn't have cared less about
who got hurt — I needed a larger field of operations than
our mission with its dismal choice between creating scandal among prudes or persecuting the helpless — that's
when I threw off my reticence and took over Ann's market
duties which meant consorting more and more with Hester —

Once in town as a regular identity I began to care what our neighbours thought of me and accordingly soiled my clothes and loosened my hair — Louisa was the only one able to note these changes without censoring me — I used the succulent vegetables we produced as bait to lure victims my way in Yandilli high street where for every sixpence worth we sold I delivered a diatribe against the commoner sins — backed up by Hester —

We became known as the vegetable people — local gardeners envied our skill — and according to legend people surreptitiously invoked our name when planting their crops — but this was a wicked liberty —

Then strange plants were belatedly found sprouting in the region — fleshy little knobs appearing harmless enough along the roadside until some child pricked its thumb and they were diagnosed as cactuses — soon to bud extra knobs like puffy fingers on a puffy hand — a visiting botanist from Amsterdam declared them a pest and within a week was proved right because they turned out to be prickly pear — an acknowledged curse up north along the Hunter River — in next to no time they grew waist-high — so dense that they choked the pastures and surrounded farmhouses all along the valley from Yandilli to Bunda — which naturally did not include our property — we took two sulkies and drove down to view them one Saturday afternoon — speechless at the sight of paddle-shaped growths crowding by the thousand round the walls of a cottage — they clustered like the heads of a rioting mob swarming in from all sides to besiege the place and chase the owners away — the house stood silent and abandoned — we were told the starved cattle had been driven elsewhere — "What for?" I asked querulously "so they can spread the pest wider in their droppings?" —

This was considered both indecent and malicious as I later heard —

I suppose I ought not to be surprised that farming folk felt they needed to blame somebody (we had gone through a similar process ourselves) or that they presumed the consequences of my new outgoing routine would prove ever more noxious until I succeeded in corrupting and bankrupting the entire community — and maybe it *was* I for instance who drove the Roman Catholic congregation to ever more frenzied pagan lapses of female-worship so they paraded their idol (a thing of painted lips human hair and clattering beads) down to the wharf and back to church — who is to say? — and maybe it *was* I who lured the new outlaws to ever more clandestine plots against the young Queen Victoria's legitimate interests —

God knows I suffer enough —

Although our own confessionals were back in full operation no one dared touch me — regardless of the admissions and imprecations I called out and the penances I inflicted on myself for the failure of our hens to lay or for a pimple disfiguring Elizabeth's nose or for the hardness of the timber we split as firewood or even for a change in the wind — my crimes were so endless I insisted on all-night chronicles till I had no strength to stand and sobbed myself to exhaustion admitting it all though nobody wanted to hear me out — I begged them to forgive me because I believed the same as they believed and it never crossed my mind we might be mistaken in our faith — so while they accused each other I accused myself — but only now does it occur to me that sometimes they were lying as I was and that not so many things had gone wrong really.

No! the nonsense about me being a witch was started by superstitious children in Cuttajo — you mustn't believe a word of it — the only power I have of this kind is the eagle eye — given me by God — a chance gift beyond my control — like my knowledge of the most ancient times when Earth broke open and the first humans crawled out among the plants of Eden (Eden means "the world of plants" according to the dead Beatrice) well this accounts for the tree-demons we found — I never told Mr Moloch but there was an occasion when a demon came my way and I used the eagle eye to stop it in its tracks long enough to get a good look — taking account of it as a leafy thing with a feathered tail and with grass growing along its shoulders — I dared it to stay though up until then the creature had not noticed me — it stopped stepping high steps and a clump of grass fell off — then without further ado began to turn into a human being — horrible!

You still have such curly hair! such capable hands! —
I hope I am not keeping you?

Your horse? yes I have been thinking about your horse
and so has Louisa because I see her at the well drawing a
pail of water for it right now so you need have no worries
on the horse's account — isn't the weather appallingly
dry! the whole bush a tinderbox ready to go up at the
least spark.

One way or another Louisa was a puzzle to the rest of
us (a fresh cup? sugar? cream?) for a start she came from
God knows what kind of family and then there was the
question of why she stayed with us once she found she
had to cope with a "grisly" wife —

But I suppose I am not telling you anything really
unless you understand the burden we bore in those days —
the burden I've been explaining — our power to injure
and destroy (though the injuries and destruction we came
to be accused of were nothing to do with us) — prior to
my loss and my outburst this had been a matter we de-
voutly begged God to lift from our shoulders — He declined in His infinite wisdom so we had to face up to our
duty and submit to punishment —

Before Immanuel was born I remember hundreds of
occasions when I stood before my husband's judgement
while he summoned others to witness what I said and
then talked quietly to me in a wheedling tone which I
knew would set them going until sure enough a response
came — from Elizabeth Canning in her wheelchair per-

haps — in the same cajoling mode with echoes of similar references to love — assuring me of my place among the Chosen — but soon rising in pitch at the mention of a leak in the shed roof maybe or the persistence of her own headache — and by this time let me say her face would be reaching right up against mine with her eyes wide and her mouth agape for me to feel the heat of her rage on my skin before her claws raked at my hair as she tugged my head back or the jolt when she hit me while she screeched accusations that I had become host to evil spirits endangering everybody by giving the Devil house room oh yes this was my life and proof of my wicked influence because soon afterwards others would join in a chorus beating me down on to the carpet demanding nothing less than perfection — you may say all this was behind me and yet it remained vividly in memory —

So now that my turn had come I don't mind telling you I made the most of it — the fact is that people grow more vicious the worse their illness until they are little better than beasts by the time their ravaged bodies are dragged to the brink of death — the only thing holding them back is weakness —

I became the one — when the show was over — to bring cups of cocoa and digestive biscuits for the others — to help them up and stroke their hands while they drank — you have no idea — in a way it was like singing in a choir and losing yourself in the harmony — you felt so refreshed afterwards.

Mr Moloch left us in 1880 when there were still seven

ladies here — Louisa Edwina Hester Ann Lavinia — who have I missed? — did I say Edwina? — yes — Elizabeth Canning and myself — yet within a year poor dim-witted Lavinia took a turn for the worse and Elizabeth was already bedridden — sad times —

I could never accept Hester's theory that the consumption was a symptom of faith — "Where does that leave my recovery?" I demanded to know —

When we told Mr Moloch he had to go — this tremendous thing we did — Louisa Theuerkauf took it upon herself to show us we could not only handle his machines and tools but make the decisions —

Some said that without either a boy to trap rabbits or a man to shoot kangaroos we would never manage for meat but Louisa encouraged Hester to practise until she became a better shot than Mr Moloch and eventually this saved the mission a tidy sum in wasted cartridges because she didn't need to bother keeping in practice — meanwhile the rest of us turned drudgery to our own advantage and discovered new freedoms hammering and puttying and mowing so that at night in the dormitory we began to exchange stories about our families — previously we would never have dared because this was the very stuff of our spiritual spying —

Yet still — for some reason — we left Louisa out and made her sleep in the room she had commandeered for herself when we first arrived —

Even so we allowed her to take part in the history we

began to compile — beginning with Judge Honeywood and the voyage — the aerial battle — and including her own vivid account of being drowned and chasing the demons —

"Those feather masks!" I cried out with a shudder and Louisa smiled at me — yes she smiled —

In my case they have never lost their terrifying power because they come out of a man's imagination and they are very foreign to anything a woman might dream up — even when I think of the masks as masks and the demons as natives (even bringing to mind my memories of their jolly wives) I am not really reassured — they still surround me in nightmares from time to time which is curious when you think how often I am out among them these days besides having a real affection for the wives — nothing to do with any rumoured witchcraft let me say.

I have no doubt you are right and that this does make me unpopular with people in town but I have decided upon my new mission and I do what I do because at last (with Louisa's help) I have fathomed God's purpose in sending me here and putting me through all the torture of grand hopes and deception to reach a stage of wisdom where I can laugh at myself — as the legless Elizabeth used to say "No extra dumplings for taking the solemn view!" to which Edwina had a standard response "It is only a matter of life and death after all!"

May I freshen your cup?

I suppose I never felt my position did justice to my

abilities or insight until I was told I carried the divine child — which may be why I came to believe — though I am sure I do not wish to sound the least bit complacent — before then it was a case of battling against the current simply because the current existed — more like an instinct than a policy.

Well for a start I mean against evil thoughts which resulted in being haunted by the flutter of insect wings and by something touching me after dark with feelers I imagined as long as your arm — besides by such nuisances as encroaching creepers taking over the whole mission so that hard as one fought them back by day they burgeoned in the knowledge of our abilities and grew while we slept — until any morning you might find their long shadows reaching in again to trespass on your bed —

I include the wider problem of the bush surrounding us with its infestation of little hairy legs and its plague of champing jaws and microscopic couplings especially in this parish — especially in those days — because I assure you rank fertility was rife enough then to be smelt on the breeze like sour skin —

Who was to doubt the cause while we remained a community of ladies? — what else should we expect but an invasion by these wasted teemings and swarmings in pursuit of anyone who might conceivably be thought fair game for the Devil? — but do pardon me — a man investigating murder scarcely needs reminding that the entire bush is overheated or the bounty of it! the wonder is

that there are not more rapes and sonnets than there are —
and that the burghers of Bunda don't come crawling up
here on hands and knees to sniff round in their droves —

Mark my words — all we are doing in this place is
returning — trying to make a journey back to the innocence we can never find again at home — don't ask me
why —

I cannot explain what a struggle it is to have to sort
among the thousands of words in my head for the few I
need to fit the case.

Did that door creak? I suspect so though your ears
should be sharper than mine but it is all we can expect
considering the traditions of this house — the peeping
and listening in — so I shall not care a jot — I used to
be driven mad but now I refuse to bother — go ahead
whoever you are! don't consider me! — mind you I know
some secrets of my own though we ought not to mention
them just here and now.

Maybe you have occasionally felt real demons brush
past unseen with their itchy clothing and hot lewdness —
you know what I'm saying? (be an angel and pass me that
cushion will you?) well despite this I don't doubt that
the natives here do sometimes *mean* to be taken for demons — though for a long while I could not be sure why
my husband had pranced about offering to fight them —
did he believe in them or not? — what of the possibility
that their paint was intended to look simply festive? —

Though personally I would never be foolish enough to take any natives for granted — especially painted ones who are pretty sure to be up to no good for the very reason that they have painted themselves — let me not preach to the converted — there is nothing more interesting than art because it can be understood — whereas religion goes on baffling us —

Did he believe they were demons? —

That was the question that dogged me —

Doubts lodged in my mind since Mr Moloch was famous for being able to recognize Satan anywhere and I had never seen him behave in such a way before — far from bouncing around with his fists up he usually froze on the spot — so for example one might be in a city street seeing him stiffen for no apparent reason — or one might be watching sailors scamper down the rigging like monkeys or a single man at Yandilli wharf stand up from where he had been seated on a bollard and Mr Moloch going rigid like a dog catching a scent — the frequency of these contacts simply demonstrated how thoroughly rotten society had grown and how close at hand the Second Coming must surely be —

So I won't let you poke fun at Mr Moloch —

I shall never forget Beatrice telling me how one morning in Stroud she saw a grey bird flutter down out of the sky to settle on his hand and leave a gold ring there which he wore as God's sign for his mission till the day he left us though I'm blessed if I know what has happened to it since — despite the festering doubts —

I have to confess that perhaps I still do believe in the prophet's message — most of what he said is confirmed in the Scriptures — you remember the man coming up out of the midst of the uttermost sea in Deuteronomy eighteen? —

One night he came rushing from his hut demanding to know how Satan had found him here — considering that as Nicodemians we followed Christ in strict secrecy — and with wild looks informed us at the time when we had set sail for Australia the only person to be told our true destination was Judge Honeywood — in days gone by an intimate of the great Joanna Southcott who believed she was pregnant with the Holy Ghost and died giving birth to nothing — though this by no means disproved her claim — so the judge could not be suspected of breathing a word to anybody — oh no! —

My husband questioned us — had he not guarded our secrecy in the chapel without windows? had he ever given way to the temptation to seek notoriety or praise for himself? — and I confess my eyes filled while I felt the old guilt rise because in my heart I honoured him as the young man who led me through a tannery to show that I could survive even Hell with his guidance as long as I was told the truth and only the truth.

Looking back a lifetime later?

Yes he failed in what he believed he was to do — yes of course that's true — but perhaps from the greatness of his belief rather than the smallness of his spirit and one has to admit he always insisted that he of himself was nothing — which we put to the test eventually when we invited him to leave the mission and without a murmur he went back to his trade as a bootmaker —

An interesting trade because shoes do grow to be part of a person as no other article of clothing does — is it too farfetched do you think to claim that shoes wear into the shape of our character? — you will know how if you have ever worn someone else's — this was the prophet's belief which he demonstrated by inviting us to exchange shoes with each other — I defy anybody to explain the strange message of the wrong foot shape or the way it conflicts with the way one stands and what that means —

"The message of the simple shoe" my husband explained "is like the riddle of a prophecy — the meaning must be felt because it cannot be described" — from which he would go on to another of his favourite sayings "Those who need descriptions will never rest content until they reform the world — whereas when Jesus returns he will instantly destroy and just as instantly rebuild it — what's more we shall be privileged to witness this because we are living the last days!"

We looked forward to a future which would obliterate the past forever — there was only one thing Mr Moloch wished to rescue of the past — he was convinced he had connections with an ancient family — hence his original journey to see Judge Honeywood whose mother had been the daughter of an earl and was — so the prophet said — his own grandmother around whom he built a kind of fairy tale in which the poor boy in rags who feels himself born to more chivalrous things finds he is a prince indeed — consider Moses and Jesus being raised in secret — by the bye now I have mentioned chivalry Mr Moloch insisted that God speaks as often to women as to men.

Precisely — the Voice.

Judge Honeywood's daughter told me the judge was an authority on Chinese calligraphy and quite famous apart from his duties on the bench — I cannot say how he took the notion of being related to my husband.

Oh the fact that Mr Moloch may well be *mad* is no more an argument against his prophecies than Joanna Southcott's imagined pregnancy was against hers — I am sure the Honeywoods would not have thought so either!

Wasn't I about to tell you how the killing itself happened?

Immanuel disappeared and Ann made efforts to comfort me because she had withdrawn the gruff person she used to be but I accused her of dishonesty because I wanted to hear nothing but disasters — having been brought to understand the full extent of the boy's danger now he was no longer a divine child assured of God's protection — you may imagine how sick at heart I felt — how soiled — how disgusted by my credulity — and beyond everything how worried for his safety — like any normal mother I pictured him being butchered by escaped convicts —

We immediately set out in the rain —

For three days that rain continued to pour down in relentless torrents creating throughout the forest a strange dim light made up of gleaming fragments mirrored by dripping leaves while we plodded deep into the wildest places to search every gully we came upon (ourselves in fear of being lost) soaked to the skin and calling the whole while — mocked by our own forlorn voices — eventually trailing home at night bedraggled and aching with bitterness until on the third day Louisa shook off her fatigue to remind us of the Scriptures and what the third day meant to the risen Christ —

This enraged my husband —

I actually feared he had lost his reason so wildly did he dash himself against the trees and punch his own head when no doubt he really wished to attack her — a profound mistake because quite apart from frightening her he let her see him for what he was — Louisa's mould of flesh set to marble while his frenzy played itself out — then having assured herself he was calm enough to understand she addressed him in a stony public voice "Was it my own body with no life left already that you loved?"

He lost his last shred of power and lost it forever — what came to my mind was the text he often quoted with such relish "The House of the Dead is the place of birth" and to think I always considered it meaningless!

In fact we did find the boy that third day —

We followed a stream to its source — wading knee

deep in swirling water — clambering up over boulders — we reached a hidden clearing high in the jungle where the rocks were as overgrown with lichen as a Gloucestershire church — here Immanuel stood on a flat slab of stone — deep in conversation — speaking to a creature with its back to us though you may be sure such a wild thing had heard us coming and declined to turn round for its own reasons.

Forgive me — I shall be all right — in a moment —

Neither did it turn round a few seconds later when the smile faded from my son's face as he caught sight of us emerging among rain-drenched ferns — I say "it" because the poor soul was so little like a human or in any way decent — at this point I distinctly heard Louisa say under her breath "Shoot!" (she was right behind me) and distinctly heard this order followed by a tiny sound — a sound which made me shudder — excuse excuse me — the mechanical click of a gun being cocked — immediately a frightful bang went off leaving a stink of gunpowder —

Immanuel watched us with great dark eyes —

The wild thing still with its back to us watched Immanuel —

We watched them both —

How my heart stopped when the Voice repeated *The Lord is with you* and I remembered that John the Baptist had been a wild man —

Some fumbling went on behind me — the gun clicked

again — meanwhile silence billowed among those prehistoric trees lasting for such a terribly long-held breath
I realized we were saved — the second terrible bang shattered everything — and the anger seizing me was that
childish anger against the whole world — the creature
dropped like a sack of bones —

I cannot explain why none of us had turned in time to
prevent Mr Moloch having another try — and I accept
blame being the only one left (apart from Louisa who tells
me she was merely disgusted by the wild man when she
made her comment *"Schutt"* meaning "rubbish" so I believe) — there you have it — eighteen years have passed
since Muley Moloch committed his crime.

That is your answer — and I suddenly saw why people
thought him weaselish —

I don't know how you found out there had been a
murder at all but I am glad to get it off my chest — you
must promise me you will be gentle with him — he is
older than his years and quite frail — I'm sure I could
never live down the pain of being the one to put him in
if I didn't think you would hear me out and understand
how much an accident it was — although it looked like
murder the poor man never intended it to be murder.

The truth is that if we are to be any use tomorrow we
have to accept what happened yesterday — so you may
be sure there's something amiss when one hears so much
about what we will do in the future while there's never
a peep about what we have already done —

But I cannot talk to you any more — I'm too choked up.

I don't doze off exactly — I simply lose little bits of time — for instance I can be busy with something and then find I am doing the same thing but facing the other way.

Ann was the last to die though in her case it was not consumption nor even cancer really — she died of humiliation — that fluff of white beard did it though for my part I assure you it was rather sweet in its way — quite a bush with a moustache to match — she felt she could never show her face in the street without being frightfully stared at so it was no wonder she stayed home and hid indoors — she said she even caught *us* staring —

Dearest of all she scolded me to cover how much she loved me —

Dying in her bed she gradually degenerated into an old man — her plump face hollowed out to the ridges and pockets of her skull — lips stretched so thin across big teeth that she got into the habit of licking them as if feeling to be sure they were still there — she had shown me so many kindnesses during my life that I could not bear the thought of living without her which is probably why I could think of nothing appropriate or comforting to say and why her distress irritated me so much I found it actually distasteful to be with her —

She wanted me to hold her hand and tell her about Heaven — instead of which I criticized her for not getting up — I chafed her wrists — I threw open the window and let the blinding sunlight in and demanded answers to my questions about how much she had improved since the day before — oh dear me.

I sometimes see myself — I am standing at a table and nothing at all is happening except that the knife in my hand has sliced an onion in two — the kitchen is rich with meanings so is the onion and so is the knife — I feel my heart will break for the joy of seeing my part in the great human tragedy while our clock makes the tremendous effort of ticking and the big hand trembles jerkily from minute to minute though the hour hand remains collected and steady —

Other times I see myself reaching out towards my young son while he shrinks — I am remembering how grief-stricken I was when he lost the power of speech although as soon as he recovered it he used it to wound me — I don't believe that that boy had any idea what I suffered or that I have suffered since because I saw him suffering — then and there in the jungle he needed nobody to tell him the man who lay dead at his feet was an Englishman — nor the reason why Mr Moloch threw away his gun and burst out with "I am the one who wanted the world to be a good place!"

One day Sergeant Arrell you will wake to find you have grown old and this will be the day when you realize time does not pass — it accumulates — there is such a lot of it blocked up in me I can hardly move —

The point is that when my husband fired the fatal shot he couldn't have known this was a white man with the fellow so indescribably filthy and shaggy besides being completely naked and burnt by the sun —

I know we ought to have buried him but we had no tools with us — Mr Moloch took the corpse by one wrist and dragged it off among some bushes to be heaped with soggy dead leaves — then he delivered a prayer sincerely commending the fellow's soul to his Maker — after which he turned towards us and I suppose despite the rain we *had* assembled in the usual way ready to listen — he confessed that maybe this was not the only man whose soul he put in jeopardy "So I give back the name of Muley Moloch to Muley Moloch — and pray the Lord God Almighty that no one should suffer punishment for my sins but myself alone" he said "I shall again take the name my father gave me" —

It has to be admitted that he did not report the death when we returned — which was wrong — and so this spelt the end of the mission as it had been — the end of our decent place and the end of our great secret — though we went on living together —

Illness transformed the remaining Hidden Stars one by one — Elizabeth Canning losing her pained look of a cripple to be touched by the beauty of childhood — doubt creeping into Hester's perpetual carping to entirely take over — while Charlotte shed her familiar gentle character and emerged as a ravaged tyrant —

These precious friends took to their beds — each in

turn — and died lonely deaths — mostly of the consumption as I have already explained — though in Lady Edwina's case it was a seizure which at first paralysed her down one side and then took her altogether — until in ninety-five my dearest Ann's turn came — the sadness makes a mockery of our hopes really.

Mr Moloch had long since gone to re-establish himself in his trade so Louisa and I had to bury Ann's corpse unaided — being the only ones left —

We were presented with the problem of making her decent — you will recall what a large person she was and we did find her a terrible handful — experienced though we both were and efficiently as we worked on either side of the bed — first we stripped and sponged her ready for arranging her in her best ironed clothes and dressing her hair — well I had only just begun wiping one bulbous white leg when the feel of that dead flesh made me qualmy — the nerveless rubbery weight of it I suppose — I don't know — but apparently my weakness showed because I found Louisa watching me and realized that this was a Louisa who had put off her customary cold reserve like a wrap no longer needed —

Having counted a little too much on my strength I now understood that so had Louisa because her eyes were clouded with tears and it cost her an effort to hold them back — impossible tears — well — from this moment I knew she could be reached and that I was not doomed to live wholly alone and that much as I would miss Ann with her lovable grumbling God was providing somebody to remain here with me — to help with my work among the natives — I won't say I realized He was providing somebody for me to grow fond of — which came later — but company at least —

I asked her whether or not my husband had ever made love to her (you may not believe it but this is how bluntly I opened the subject) — she gave the matter some thought while attending to the corpse and gravely wiping the left leg as I wiped the right before straightening it out — "No" she replied — unless I wished to count his miracle in bringing her back from the dead —

I caught myself imagining her there on the bed in place of the corpse — her limbs might look much like Ann's and her flesh might feel as solid and cool under my hand — I imagined her *being* the corpse until for a horrid fleeting moment I experienced a flicker of the interest Mr Moloch might have had in her —

We sponged Ann's poor feet with their bunions and dried between the toes — I glanced up at her face and I could have sworn I caught her breathing — but no — then we shook the folds from a petticoat still warm with the cupboard smell and heaved and hefted and tugged at the unwilling cloth to get it over her head — pulling it down — difficult because her skin was damp —

Miserably flushed and with our hair flopping loose we struggled at the task of restoring decency — although finally brutally we found we had to bounce the body when we came to work the dress over its hips and pull the stuff straight — by the time we came to brush her hair and coil her bun as she liked it we were wrecks —

Over a cup of tea the full awfulness of marriage seemed suddenly obvious to me — the folly of respectability and knowing one would rather *die* than be made a fool of — the revulsion I felt in that instant was against my own jealousy and against the useless pain of having lived so many years in the grip of suspicions —

After resting we worked together once more attending to the matter of plugging our friend's ears and nostrils with little balls of cloth — then we hoisted her head and shoulders on to some planks set in position to slope down from the top step into the waiting sulky — as we bent to ease her on to this slope I recalled the attitudes of stooping men scouring skins at the tannery and the way they had glanced up at me from under their brows and the vile thoughts they had obviously thought — her head thudded with a painless impact —

I was trembling from exhaustion by then and so was Louisa but we still had much to do and drove together up to the graveyard without a word while something happened between us and the mounting turbulence urgently rising to choke me was — I believe as I look back on it and despite the occasion — joy!

We buried her up there with the others — you should be able to see the crosses — yes — all our bodies have been buried in the one patch — our Hidden Stars.

I wished Mr Moloch had been with us for the sake of his authority at funerals and to lend a helping hand because as it was we undid a lot of our good work by dirtying her dress and making a mess of her hair — yet the grave we had dug was adequate and she lay in it looking relieved while I delivered a service in my own way — then Louisa sang a strange beautiful melody to Latin words (which I hoped did not come from the Catholic mass but found so moving I dared not interrupt even for the sake of rescuing a dead friend's soul) I underwent my usual irrational anxiety in case the corpse might not truly be dead and only in a coma of apoplexy or partial suffocation — it had been the same ever since I felt we ought not to leave Beatrice among those stones on Ascension Island —afterwards we dropped flowers in and covered her with a blanket —

We would miss her — we would miss her strategic discontent —

We were too weak to unbuckle straps when we got back home so we left the pony in harness and plumped ourselves on the edge of the well with heads bowed to recover our broken breath — wheezing horribly I reached out on impulse to touch Louisa's hand as she had once reached out to touch me when I was pregnant — to my astonishment she grasped it firmly and drew me towards her — she folded me in her arms so the smell of our stale labours mingled and for a moment we clung there as survivors of a shipwreck —

I knew then that I was so free from Muley Moloch it would make no difference whether or not I saw him again — that he might even come back someday to live out his old age — I could employ Louisa as my house-keeper and let her take him in for a lodger once we partitioned the old dormitory into several rooms — suddenly I was full of plans.

More and more I find myself dreaming of England and the most common dream is a winter morning with fresh snow lodged on bare branches while a dozen rooks flap away toward a spinney of elms across the valley just beyond the farm fence — it is one of those days when everything seems old — yet I am walking hand in hand with Dora listening to the soft crunch of snow under our boots — we look back to see something of our character in the footprints as if time has hesitated to let us keep hold of actions just lost — I am wearing gloves and so is she yet I can feel the shape of her bony fingers through the wool and her warmth as well — we carry Bibles in our free hands and we are in no hurry to reach the Hall having set out early on purpose — the sky rests old gentle close and grey on a land crusted with crystal and I am tremendously happy so I pray to God never to let me forget one iota of this feeling which includes a special reverence for the little church in the village away to our left at the foot of the long hill — an extremely old church built of the same grey stone as the cottages with a square tower rising high above the surrounding roofs and we can even see little dots of snow on top of its spiked crown as well as the finest white eyebrow above each arched window — or at least I can see this and I am sorry for darling Dora because she cannot — Dora who has near-sight explains that though she *sees* the village she can't make out anything *of* it but she appreciates what I tell her because after all there is nothing new in what I describe — which brings me to stop in awe at having the first important idea of my life —

"Catherine dear!" she gasps and alarm fills her eyes "are you ill?" —

I am not at all ill — I am simply unable to put words to my thought without destroying it altogether so I let go of her hand and place a woolly finger on my lips to keep her from speaking till I have time to get used to what being clever means (I can describe this now but oh my goodness it was difficult then) my idea is that there might be no such thing as a real village or a real any-thing — because while I look across the valley and see a village clearly Dora can look inward to what she knows by memory and see the same village every bit as clearly — which surely makes her idea as real as my solid stone! —

When we walk on we are no longer as happy as we were though I have the advantage of being a superior creature —

So Dora sulks and pilots us to the side of the road where she can kick at some frosty tufts of grass and trample a

frozen cobweb but she is only angry because I have shut
her out so her anger flatters me and by the time we reach
the gate I am positively triumphant — I tell her I love
the way these stone gateposts lean and the way the stone
caps on them have worn (especially the one with a diagonal
crack) — when some imp in my brain tempts me to make
a show of opening the gate for her to put her even more
at my mercy so I dart over to the latch and grasp the
great wooden beam of the top bar but she sees more than
I do — she sees my motive as well as my action and
refuses to be humiliated —

With the energy and boyishness of a much younger
girl she manages her skirts and climbs the gate to swing
over and leap down on the other side before I have a
chance to let myself through — so now I am the one who
is cross because she won't allow me to enjoy an idea
without having to tell her about it — this means I am
no longer blissfully happy yet I still want to be — which
must be why I clash the gate behind me and run up to
her and begin dusting the snow off her clothes after her
escapade — all the while scolding her for the scalliwag
she has become —

Being called a scalliwag pleases her immensely and we
pause a moment at the roadside on the brink of an ice-
crusted ditch while a trap comes bowling along the road
and the gentleman in it raises his hat though we giggle
because we do not recognize him and we know he has
come a long way since his horse's flanks are smoking —

then when he is out of sight we gaze across at the ivy-grown wall of the gatehouse and remark on the curiosity that no snow has collected on this ivy so we decide like a committee that the wind must have come from the north-east or this wall would not be so sheltered — old bare trees tower over the gatehouse and among their net of twigs looms the Hall with its chimneys — stone chimneys having lozenge patterns carved on some and twisted candy braids on others — I point out the peacock perched at the peak of one roof with his tail dusting the snowy slates and ask Dora humbly where peacocks come from — "China" she replies without hesitation and kisses my cold cheek —

Having crossed the road we push through a squeaky iron turnstile at the side of the gatehouse to make our way up the broad gravel drive enchanted at finding the snow has moulded the judge's garden to smooth simple forms — like an outward expression of my soul at that moment — with clipped hedges of evergreens carrying domes of snow and the sundial standing on a perfect oval carpet where the star of pathways converges — statues of heroic figures in plumes and armour lean on shields or broadswords — mature yew trees gather all the shadows of that bright place into their rich recesses and broad shallow semicircular steps lead down to a frozen pond beyond which the grand old house stands gazing over its domain through majestic windows —

Miss Honeywood is waiting for us because there has

been a scandal in the village and she intends to learn everything she can from us before the cottagers' children troop in for Sunday School — the scandal being that a notorious poacher called Giles Coney who once ravaged the woods in the eighteen-twenties until he was caught and transported to New South Wales has returned after serving his sentence and the point is that he has cut a great figure in the district by showing the welts on his back to some drinkers at the White Hart and swearing to break every bone in Judge Honeywood's body for having sentenced him — even if the luxury of this revenge costs another sentence and the rest of his life back in the colonies in chains —

We have heard my Uncle Herbert on the subject so we are able to assure her that this is indeed what the creature said —

We sit either side of her fireplace in the small wainscoted parlour watching logs crackle and the glow reflected by panelled wood — our noses and ears are pink and we sniff politely while enjoying the comfort of warmth — we feel very close and very happy because Mr Coney's threats are nothing to do with us and we have never even seen Miss Honeywood's father so how can we imagine what it might be like for him to be in danger? — then I am surprised again by the logic of my original idea concerning the village as I saw it and as Dora imagined it —

Because this logic must apply to everything in the world —

Is the real brutality suffered by a criminal more real than the ideal suffering one may imagine when hearing about it just because it is more painful — any more than the real discomfort of influenza is more serious than the evil thoughts by which somebody else may cause it to strike?

I have worried a good deal along these lines since then (especially since coming out here and eventually learning that we could no longer rely on Mr Moloch for guidance) well we should remember the pious Wesleyan preacher's estimate that every twenty years each of us is likely to commit six hundred and forty-nine million sins — any one of which would be grave enough to ensure eternal damnation — so where does that place us in respect of a man caught poaching and sent for fourteen years in chains? —

Never let it be said that coming events do not cast their shadows before them — or that our true life is not lived through memories.

Thank you Louisa you may bring the sandwiches now — we are firm believers Sergeant in the healthful properties of a sandwich taken with a glass of water.

I rejected England you see and so did the rest of the Stars who came out here to help create the New Jerusalem for one reason or another which I do not wish to go through in detail — but there is a profound difference between this and the case of a Giles Coney being spurned *by* England although I could not condone the man's lawlessness (since he belonged in Cold Dean which was a village I knew) I do claim that even in the case of crimes more serious than poaching the causes may not be as simple as they appear —

Did I mention that the man's left wrist was badly scarred or that he had certainly been a convict? no — not Mr Coney — the wild man.

What I suppose I am saying is that our worst offences are often overlooked and nothing in my life fills me with such horror as the thought of my husband stealthily using me while I was unconscious — despite the fact that he would always have been welcome when I was awake — so I cannot tell whether or not this also stood between me and Immanuel though I believe I felt the same love as any mother has for her child —

Let me confess that in order to allow my husband to disappear and start a new life we reported him lost at sea — well it was only a white lie because he very nearly had been — then just as soon as I inherited the property I cast off his surname in the same ceremonial way he had cast off Muley Moloch's name — I went back to being Catherine Byrne as I had been when I fell in love with Dora and when she fell in love with a strange man who didn't even notice her but who floated up off the floor for me —

We let the lawn go to pot —

There was never any mention of whether Giles Coney had scars on his wrist as well as his back but until we heard of his return to the district I don't believe I had given a thought to New South Wales so I suppose this is what put the idea in my head — ready for when I suggested it on my wedding day as a way out of suggesting a mission to China!

Yes I believe one day my faith will be restored to me but it cannot be hurried because there is no point in chasing after faith — faith comes or does not come and when it does it is always as a gift to the undeserving — so although one should never indulge one's wickedness it is no use imagining one can ever *earn* faith by good works — I am tremendously down on good works — and who among us can truthfully say his life is not a battle against his nature?

What else should I confess to you while I have the chance to influence the way you judge all this? I'd like to flush the whole lot out of my system in the interests of fairness to Mr Moloch — because he is the one who still needs help —

For a start I ought to clear Louisa of all responsibility — she had nothing to do with anything and she was in no position to overhear what Immanuel told me after the murder so she could never have guessed the victim was one of us — apart from which she is my employee these days — as I say — so I take responsibility for her provided she cooks and minds the cats when I am out because I spend a good deal of time in Yandilli — occasionally I drive as far as Bunda for the Sunday service — nor must you hold it against her that her saying is "It's time for women to be led by women" because who can be sure whether she means it or not? —

You might be interested to hear that her singing voice sounds as clear as ever though I happen to know she is fifty-seven but please don't let slip the least hint that I told you or that she has the curious habit of stretching her lips to cover her teeth whenever she opens her mouth wide —

Louisa never learned the piano you know despite having a certain skill at vamping accompaniments — when there is any serious playing to be done I am dragooned into service though she is terribly critical of my abilities — she has even given me some singing lessons because of our little secret — recently I have begun learning a new piece which she was engaged to perform when she was supposed to return to Germany years ago and never went — it's a duet — and though we have no music she remembers both parts (mine was intended for a tenor so I take it up an octave) — since she has taught me this strange modern composition — I have it completely by heart — everything else begins to sound artificial by comparison *"O sink hernieder Nacht der Liebe!"* — glorious yet simple — and because we have no piano part we can sing it while working in the garden or walking through the forest down to the main road now a road has at last been put through *"Herz an Herz dir Mund an Mund"* or my little solo bit that goes *"zu täuschendem Wahn entgegenge-*

stellt" (do you have any German?) "Heart on heart and lip on lip we defy the delusions of the world" very sad — "make me forget I live" so haunting — Louisa describes it as peaceful music which makes me wonder about her — though in a curious way it *is* peaceful —

Human pride is a terrible thing when you come to think about Louisa accepting a contract to tour the Antipodes simply because Mr Wagner was only going to cast her as Isolde's understudy in his new piece — but of course she adored him and she was young —

The cats? yes there are five cats and since we put the fence between our two houses they have taken to staying over there more often than living with me although they were originally mine but I do not begrudge Louisa in the light of everything she has given up — make no mistake about it to turn one's back on fame must be a tremendous sacrifice not to mention the loss of that peculiar satisfaction said to be unique to artists when they perform — really it was thinking of this that I set out to become her friend once Ann passed away — in the beginning she was thrust upon us as a disaster and yet eventually you could say Miss Theuerkauf became the one to set us free —

It makes me wonder if there might have been enlightened souls among the convicts too — I mean we simply do not know what talents have been lost — convicts must be born like anyone else with their share of native wit — some mute inglorious Milton here may rest — here — some youthful genius stifled and taught only how to

die — A youth to Fortune and to Fame unknown — and
so forth — do you recognize it? — Heaven did a recom-
pense as largely send — He gave to Misery all he had (a
tear) — He gained from Heaven (twas all he wished) a
friend — the lovely lovely lines of dear Gray —

Incidentally if anyone was ever victorious in death that
would have to be Ann Whittaker who surely flew straight
to the arms of Jesus —

Did I tell you how Immanuel ran away again while we
were busy covering the wild man's corpse? and that no
one noticed? well the last I saw of him was his cheeks
going purple as he stood goggling down at the dead man
before screaming in Mr Moloch's face "He looked after
me!" — this was why we decided to leave the boy to his
own devices until we finished the job as best we could
with a mound of leaf mulch — we called him when we
were ready to start out on our way back down the creek
but he was simply nowhere to be found — though we
called and called among those mossy jungle trees there
was no answer except whispers beginning all about us and
continuing high above — no sound of fleeing footfalls or
sign of the child who was to have saved the world and
reigned in majesty for a thousand years — nothing but
a multitude of whispers —

I never saw him since — but I think of him lovingly
every minute of the day —

He did write to me once from the Ballarat so I dare
say we can thank Digby Barnett and the habitual Barnett

failures for Immanuel thinking he might pick up a fortune in the street there (though I don't mean to include young Barney who has been a great help lately) but in all justice I dare say we do the same thing in our own way while we continue to keep ourselves ready for a miraculous future —

Ten years later Immanuel sent me a letter from England which I carry next to my heart — I have it right here and I shall show it to you — just wait a tick —

Till I get — breath — "My dear Mother, I do not have anything much to say, except a powerful wish to say that this is so! Besides, I do not wish you to waste your grief on me thinking I am dead or anything so easy. I must thank you for the tales you told me when I was a child, these are what I remember, King Gundafar in particular as well as the tale of Mr Giles Coney, but I have discovered that the judge died peacefully at home so Mr Coney must now satisfy his passion by frightening Miss Honeywood instead . . . all for a brace of pheasants and a hare or two, it makes me glad to be an Australian! The occasion of my writing today is to inform you that I have spoken to my grandfather on the subject of the Empire and the changes that may soon happen with the loosening of ties, but he offered no more than to declare himself glad to hear of you alive although he does not wish to see you, so he hopes you are going to stay in New South Wales. My great-grandmother Boulton left me her house in Stroud, a very poky little place, hardly fit to live in. I dare say I

shall sell it as soon as I am able. Finally, I send my love
to Aunt Ann and wish you well. Your dutiful son, Immanuel Moloch."

Do you see what a hand he has! I taught him to write
like that! but of course he was never *Moloch* he was
Immanuel Heaps — oh dear! — and I have been trying
my best to protect us all.

We defeat ourselves.

Truth to tell I feel horribly tired.

Now you come to mention it there *were* some alarming
noises at night the Monday before last — that was Boxing
Day wasn't it? — yes and when Louisa called me quite
late I went outside to listen with her but for a long time
nothing else happened — it was a hot still night and the
mosquitoes were bad — we listened — hardly daring to
breathe — then we heard what sounded like a gun shot
down on the flat towards the cliffs — but of course that's
a good two miles from here — a single random pop
ominous enough to stop the heart — well we looked at
one another across the fence — I believe we relived the
same memory because Louisa's voice shook a little when
she cried "What is this?" — and it takes a lot to make
her voice shake — then the very instant the question was
out another shot sounded — at about ten or eleven
o'clock — followed by screams from the same direction — screams swallowed in silence — sucked up into
the night among the unblinking stars —

So there we were — each in our own garden — each with our piece of the divided lawn which Mr Moloch had cut that very afternoon — straining to hear what we could and afraid of believing what we knew —

Louisa hissed at me "Was she screaming *Father?*" which made me go cold all over and shiver at the thought of little Immanuel's voice (my own too) — but we caught nothing more — not even that murmur of a million spirits which sometimes drifts down from the mountain — though we waited until the mosquitoes were beyond bearing and the cats got back into her house so they had to be put out again —

We shook our heads as I recall — and very possibly the whole thing was a prank because we were warned there was to be a dance at Cuttajo hall and the sinners would be out in force for sure so the road was most likely crowded all night with young folk on their way to perdition.

Sergeant!

Do you mean to say *this* was your murder? only the other day? but when I was telling you about everything — ? I thought you meant our — well our terrible event — excuse me — yes — and I wanted you to understand.

Immanuel Heaps as I say because his father is John Heaps the Bunda bootmaker — we often drove into

Bunda on a Sunday to hear him preach privately at his house — but let me say it is quite quite impossible to suspect my poor bootmaker of violence.

How many victims? two sisters and a brother in their twenties? no no Mr Heaps is not particularly strong and we took his gun off him in any case — you say they were laid out in regulation order? how peculiar.

This is shocking! oh the poor woman! to see her children dead! there can be nothing more terrible — even the thought is a stone in the heart — can she survive such pain? — we must do something for her.

But what on earth?

Yes I *know* he left Bunda a month ago — this was because I invited him to come here and live next door as Louisa's lodger — let's not go over all that again — well perhaps because I hoped to punish her if you like! — on the night in question he was asleep in bed — you see she and I didn't go back inside for almost an hour and just when we were saying good night he appeared at the door of her place — eyes blurred — quite happily clad in nothing but his nightshirt with the weather being still so hot — he looked so little with his nose and ears bigger than ever —

I recall thinking about that nightshirt (though I knew it had to be a shop-made article and not the one sewn by Ann) and thinking these were the feet in the shoes I had once watched rising off a carpet —

When he asked what we were doing we simply waved him back to bed — no point in trying to explain to him — you see he has grown completely deaf and become a peeper — I must confess we both get a touch short on the odd occasion when we have our own worries — I wonder whether the deafness may perhaps be connected with going bald — my only objection to a bald head is the way a man's scalp wrinkles when he tilts his head back —

The oddest thing of all to a person brought up in a family believing in the absolute ugliness of evil and the absolute beauty of good is to realize that some of the ugliness was not (well not by any very serious criterion) evil at all — whereas plenty of the beauty was certainly as evil as evil — and that the way to reach this realization is through laughter —

As a matter of fact Louisa herself doesn't have much sense of humour though she is the one who puts things in such a way that others see the funny side — so she gets in quite a huff when you laugh and she can't see why — never mind —

For instance the day we buried Ann Whittaker and clung together at the well until I grew calm enough for Louisa to let me go she said "To be fearing death we are correct — " and added "only an idiot is not afraid — " she thought for a long pause — "yet each lady lying dead is like the same lady found in a different mood isn't it? — always your Ann was provincial already and a person as you say skin deep — until I help to lift up her body and feel how heavy it weighs" — despite an extremity of exhaustion this struck me as appallingly funny — though I was too polite to laugh openly —

Yet at the same time Louisa's words brought the living Ann to mind in an unexpected way because she always *had* been provincial though I'd never seen through her until that moment —

Poor Ann — did I ever understand her or what her life meant or even what her real hopes might have been or why the prophet accepted her as a disciple? — later the idea came that with her dead a bit more of that unexplained battle we once heard out in the Atlantic Ocean died also —

A bit had died with Beatrice and another bit with Lavinia and more with Edwina so that — though I kept my share — most parts were dead and buried — unless — unless Mr Moloch's deafness is a case of the real world being shut out by the need to reassemble this lost world in its entirety —

Could it be that he has been taking it back into himself all these years — fragment by fragment — cramming the whole drama into his head (does it belong there?) to be pieced together again — who knows? — perhaps when he pads around at night and appears at the door in his pyjamas — perhaps the whole thing is exploding in there — echoes booming around his skull — the dome of his disappointed life expanding to become as vast with freedom as a whole hemisphere of sky — maybe this explains why he carries his head as if balancing the weight of it — even when he shuffles along Louisa's corridor or stands at the back door — bewildered and damp — transcending his failures to become custodian of great forces locked in a raging crescendo — while his forgotten shell is left framed at the brink of an uninterrupted night — artillery guns booming without the slightest effect on cicadas or frogs — individual soldiers' groans made negligible by the universal terror and panic heard only inwardly — the bush upright and motionless with not a leaf disturbed while milling horse hooves pound the imagined Earth — the Earth a drum — the pounding relentless and chaotic — and the recollected air rent with a clamour of cries which are really neither cowardly nor heroic because they are the voices of illusion and an escape from truth —

This might explain the tension in Mr Moloch when he taps his stiff fingers on the fence rail as he is brought up short and props there without a word to anybody — or taps the table while Louisa prepares our dinner — or taps his thighs as he ambles among mementos of his failures down by the creek —

It's my belief that his body is too full of death to be able to die on its own account — and I dare say that in among the bursting shells and screaming horses he hears phrases from his sermon "Death does not destroy the *value* of life — whatever is precious is only precious by virtue of the fact that it can be lost — I do not give thanks to death because it will bring my troubles to an end — I give thanks to death because it will bring my joys and my faith to an end — " that's what he used to tell us at those passionate meetings when his face lit up with knowledge of God's word and his eyes grew big and brilliant and so dark you could lose yourself in them — "This is why we must forever fight sin and not surrender to it — because the death of sin gives meaning to sin —

Perhaps he hopes to inherit the Hall!

If there's such a thing as wisdom it comes when you realize that life is lived altogether in the imagination — each instant as it happens is already past — there is no dividing line between the window you are looking out of right now and Judge Honeywood's tall windows giving on to his park or Mrs Boulton's window dim with steam —

At times (because the world moves on and solid objects and painful afflictions become harmless souvenirs) I feel cheated — but generally I have been so strengthened by my experiences I feel I have enjoyed too much benefit and that I am an impostor.

Shall I call Louisa for you?

This frightful cough — do please excuse me — she won't be a minute.

The photographs? those indecent photographs? — well Mrs Pringle tells us that Florence Love told *her* Charles

Bailey used them not so long ago to survive the Depression — she has reason to believe he sold them in sets of six to teaching hospitals in England (here comes Louisa) so of course any thought of my ever going back home has become utterly impossible now —

But as for the future — "a new Earth wherein righteousness dwells?" — all I can say is that nothing is ever resolved — we are eternally caught waiting to be rescued — although with Immanuel in limbo and nearing thirty — do you see? — one can never tell — aha!